W. R. A. T.

By
D. J. McAllister

ISBN: 978-0-692-85617-8

Design: Dedicated Book Services, (www.netdbs.com)

DEDICATION

To all the Military Members, Veterans, First Responders, and Emergency Personnel who save our lives and protect the American People on a daily basis.

Many thanks to Betty, who without her, these books would not have been completed.

If you liked this book please post a photo of this cover on your Facebook account or other media so your friends will know where to buy this book.

AMAZON.COM / Books / djmcallister

Contents

FOREWORD

It was 1973 and the Vietnam War was continuing to be the daily bread and butter for every news show in the country. For years men were drafted and sent to Southeast Asia to fight, and sometimes, die for their country. With any of the Military Services, once your active duty time is completed and you have received a discharge, there is an inactive duty or reserve time that must be completed before you are off the hook.

There were thousands of veterans who had done their time a long time ago, but now were too old for the conflict. But since these men had the necessary experience and were already members of the reserves, they were considered excellent teachers and tutors. Many of them took their jobs seriously and rose in the ranks to be responsible leaders.

Many men had been drafted and completed their time during the early parts of the war and discharged. But they were required to complete a time in the reserve forces. I had to put my time in the reserves after I was discharged too. Fortunately I was not forced to attend all those meetings. At the time they were "over staffed"

Since there were so many United States Army Reserve (USAR) units around the country, the Army felt they needed to keep tabs on them and have a way to rate them with a grading system from bad to excellent. To do this, the decision to form teams of inspectors to travel to the Reserve unit's home station and perform the "vital" inspection was made by the Generals and Colonels in command.

The military has always used inspection teams to feel the pulse of the forces in their command. These teams have had many varied names, but always with the same charter, to tell the command what is happening in the field. Ever since there was a military, there have been military inspectors. They go together like peanut and butter.

The US Army made the decision to gin up several teams of inspectors, which were incorrectly called 'assistance teams', to check the war readiness of the USAR forces all around the country. These were to be four man teams located in the major cities within the various Army's geographical areas.

The cities to pick from in the Sixth Army area were on a short list. Albuquerque, Denver, Kansas City, Los Angeles, Omaha, Salt Lake City, San Francisco, Seattle and Wichita.

That's where I came in.

Chapter 1

Let's Put The Team Together

It looked like it would be a time of peace now after the Vietnam War, but there were still threats on the horizon and we still had to be ready. The US, North and South Vietnam and the Viet Cong signed a cease fire agreement a couple of years ago on January 27, 1973.

The war was nearly over and the troops were coming home, well most of them anyway. The last US ground troops left Vietnam on March 29th. This war had been picketed and demonstrated against right from the beginning and it was shown on the evening news like a soap opera for years.

Many Hollywood stars came out against the war. And of course, they would know because they are celebrities and the people running the war are only Generals.

I got out of the Army Signal Corps as a Spec 6 after several years and one tour over there and headed for home. I was lucky, I was in at the very end and had my fill of Vietnam, thank you very much.

I can tell you, it's a lot of fun trying to fix a radio that a GI brought in while they are shooting at you.

My boss, a full Colonel, was one of the last out. I saw a rerun of some of the video footage after I got home. There was a Huey lifting off of a roof in

Saigon, and there was a man holding onto one of the skids as it took off. That was him!

When I saw him weeks later, he laughed about it. I said, "That wasn't funny Colonel. You could have lost your grip and you'd have had a long fall down to the water."

His answer? "But I got out of there in one piece!"

Positive thinking wins every time.

I always liked hunting deer and elk in the mountains close to home. One thing about that, a little different from over there, the deer and elk didn't shoot back.

And since the Army only gave the bare essentials of training to the troops, I knew that getting an education had to be my number one priority. It's a good thing that I knew something about radio and electronics before I went in. No education, no job! Even I could figure that one out.

By some miracle, I was accepted to the University of Colorado at Colorado Springs (UCCS). I worked day night to get an Associate Degree in Electrical Engineering, and while I was in school, I studied for the FCC First Class License so there would be something to fall back on if there's not a lot of jobs around when school is over.

Well, I was right about jobs being scarce, but I got lucky and started as an engineer at a local radio station, KRDO, making a decent amount and still able to buy groceries. After two years in the radio business, I got a big break when I got a job in the Communications and Electronics (CommEl) Shop at Fort Carson as a WG-10 making more than double what

I was making an hour in radio. Do you know how much money that is? A fortune! I could buy lots of groceries now. So now, for the past two years, I've been a Department of Army Civilian (DAC), working at Fort Carson here in Colorado Springs.

When I got the job at Fort Carson, I bought a house for eleven thousand three hundred dollars. It's an old concrete block house built in 1903 on a really big lot in Fountain, a little town just south of the city. My girl friend likes to come and take care of it, and me sometimes, whenever she can, which is only about once or twice a week. Twice for the house, once for me.

Colorado Springs has to be the best place to live in the whole world. The mountains, warm days most of the time, cool nights every night, dry air all the time, hunting and fishing in the outdoors and lots of things to do here in the city. I could go on about my favorite town for hours. I can't imagine why anyone would leave here for any reason.

Not long ago, the Army made the decision to gin up several teams of inspectors, who were called 'assistance teams' to check the readiness of the USAR forces all around the country. These were to be four man teams located in the major cities within the three continental armies geographical areas. Some of the cities in the Sixth Army area listed where teams would be stationed were Omaha, Denver, Kansas City, Salt Lake, Albuquerque, San Francisco, Seattle and Los Angeles.

So in May, I decided to put in for the job since there was to be a team in Denver and one on the Post here at Fort Carson, and I was all ready and waiting here. It took a huge amount of time to get the SF-57 Federal Government Application form ready. I labored over the form every night after work for two weeks before I finally took it to the Civilian Personnel Office (CPO) and delivered it to the woman who was handling these jobs. Then it seemed like I dropped it down a sewer. I heard nothing for month after month.

However, in late September, I was notified to report on Monday the twentieth of the following month, to Salina, Kansas for an interview. Salina is about four hundred miles east on Interstate Seventy. When that Sunday came, I drove across Colorado to Oakley then on Interstate 70 to Salina.

I left about seven in the morning and it was a nice drive until I crossed the border into Kansas. The temperature rose with every mile I drove, so I stopped at Oakley for a drink and a short rest. Then Hays for another drink. By the time I arrived in Salina, I was famished.

Man! It's October and the temperature is in the high eighties and low nineties. That's August temps, not October. I couldn't take this heat for long. I was glad to find a little motel in Salina with a café and air conditioning for the night.

I met with a Lieutenant Colonel on a warm sunny Monday afternoon.

"Good afternoon, Mr. McAllister. I'm Colonel Gardner. Won't you sit down?" He said.

He pointed to a chair in front of his desk, which I promptly took and faced him.

"I have reviewed your application and resume, and I have some questions for you." He said.

"I see that you own several firearms." He said.

"Yes Sir."

"Do you have them permitted and registered?" He asked.

"Yes Sir. Every one. I use them for hunting mostly."

"Are you proficient with them?" He asked.

"Well. I can hit what I'm aiming at, if that's what you mean."

We talked for a few minutes about home and family, cars and the Army. He handed me some forms and told me to fill them out. At the bottom of the last page was a list of cities with a list of instructions to list them by preference in order of one to ten.

The list was in alphabetical order. Albuquerque, Boise, Casper, Colorado Springs, Denver, Helena, and Salt Lake. I quickly finished the list with Fort Carson first and Denver second. The rest in alphabetical order after them. Actually, I could go to any of them on the list and be happy.

I handed it back to him and waited while he studied it.

"I must have given you the wrong page here. Would you mind finishing the last question again?" He said.

The last question was the list of cities, but now the list was Bismarck, Kansas City, Lincoln, Omaha, Salina, Sioux Falls and Wichita. This is going to be tough. I didn't say it, but I don't want to be stationed in any of these cities, so I kept silent and slowly, carefully finished it and handed it back to him.

"You have omitted Bismarck, Mr. McAllister. Was that an oversight?" He asked.

"No sir. I just won't go to Bismarck."

"You're saying that if I select you for the job and it is in Bismarck that you will refuse the job?" He asked.

"Yes sir, that's right."

I felt my face flush. You just don't talk like that to a Colonel. He got a funny look on his face and dismissed me and I drove home the next day. By that time I figured it was all over for me. I won't get the job.

Well, Several months later I finally heard from CPO that I got the job and with it a big promotion to GS-9. When you are making under ten thousand dollars a year and you get a raise to twelve thousand five hundred, that's a big promotion.

The only trouble was that I was assigned to the team in Wichita! Wichita? Wait a minute! That's in Kansas! That was my number five choice! I've heard stories about Kansas weather for years from tourists who came here and some of the Army folks who were stationed at Fort Riley. And none of it was good.

I'll just go to CPO tomorrow and maybe they can help. I spent all day at CPO and the best I got was a lecture and some bad advice.

"If you want the promotion and the money, you'll have to go to Wichita to get it." The Personnel Officer said.

"Great! Just great!"

But at least they made an agreement with me that after one tour of three years, I could come home to Fort Carson and they would give me the first available vacancy on the Post that was the same grade. That probably means the same grade I am now! But it's something. I got it in writing too, if that means anything. Well, the situation looks very clear, much to my dismay. If I'm going to get anywhere working for the Army, I guess I'm going to have to go to Wichita.

Since I'm supposed to report for duty on the first Monday after New Years, I'll take off Sunday morning and make the drive down to Pueblo on the Interstate, then along the Arkansas River on Highway 50 to Dodge City and Highway 54 the rest of the way. There's no telling how things will go on this new job, so I'm not going to take everything I own right now. Besides, I really don't want to move my model railroad layout that's in the basement. My house payment is only eighty three dollars a month, and I can maintain that to be sure that I have a place to come back to if the job doesn't work out.

I have a '55 Chevy Cameo pickup that can stay here in the garage, and I'll drive my "baby", a 1965 Porsche 356S coupe. I don't need to take that much anyway, some clothes and other personal stuff is all I'll need, I think. Dad said he'd take care of the house while I'm gone.

As I was driving along US Highway 50 across southern Colorado toward Kansas, I couldn't get this song out of my mind. "Hi Ho, Hi Ho, It's off to work we go."

The towns kept ticking off. La Junta, Las Animas, Lamar, Holly, the Colorado border, Garden City, Dodge City, Greensburg, Pratt, and Kingman. Finally, there's a sign for Wichita, eighty six more miles.

When you come in to Wichita from the west, the airport is the first thing you see out there all alone on the west side. The sign says "Wichita, 5 miles". Boy, this town must be bigger than I thought. Actually, I found out later that it's about the same size as Colorado Springs. It's just arranged differently and flat, really flat. I have to find the office where I'm supposed to report, but first I need to find someplace to stay and a nice dinner. And on Sunday afternoon that might be tough.

Luckily, I found a room at the "Y" and the desk clerk directed me to a really good looking little "Mom and Pop" restaurant two blocks away, where I had catfish, no kidding, catfish and hush puppies for dinner. The waitress gave me directions to get to the office tomorrow. It's only a short drive down George Washington Boulevard, so I better drive out tonight and have a look.

Chapter 2

The Arcom

Our office is in the Eighty Ninth Army Command Headquarters (ARCOM) building way out on the southeast side next to what they told me was an Air Force base located on the old municipal airport. When I entered the building on Monday morning, no one seemed to know who I was or what to do with me.

Fortunately the head man, Tom E. Hall, knew about the program and had someone show me to our office, which for the time being was a corner of another office used by the JAG officers. And you know what it's like sitting around with a bunch of Jag Offs. That's a joke, folks. JAG stands for Judge Advocate General. They are lawyers. But they only use the room on drill nights. Well, I'm the only one on the team and no one knows when anyone else will be coming. I'm not sure anyone even knows that I'm here.

I've been here a week and have walked around and met everyone I could and tried not to look like a hippie or slovenly. I had to move 'the office' twice, but at least now I have a desk and a chair, no matter how old and unserviceable they are.

I went down the hall to talk to Mr. Hall and he gave me some phone numbers at the Sixth Army Headquarters so I can get information on our mission and any operating instructions that would be good to study while I'm waiting for the rest of the team to show up. It would be nice if I had a phone too. I used the USAR school's phone to make a couple of calls to Sixth Army HQ, but the people that I talked to out there said they didn't know anything, and said to call back. Big help!

I have been here about a week and tonight is the reserves drill night so I think I'll make a quiet visit to see what they do. Their drill starts at six pm, so I'll just get there about a quarter till and act like I know what I'm doing. Sometimes I'm not a very good actor.

I drove to the Reserve Center and quietly entered my office and tried to be as unobtrusive as I could, but I'm in civilian clothes and everyone else in dressed in fatigues and I stood out like a beacon on a dark night. It's ten after six and I'm standing in the doorway to the office and everyone is hurrying through the halls and I heard a voice that sounded like it was coming from the next office to my left.

"So you're the one with the long hair!" The voice said.

I looked to my left to see a man in his fifties with a single star on his collar standing in the doorway.

"Uh, oh." I know this can't be good. He saw me looking in his direction and waved to me.

"I'm General Masters." He said. "Come on in and sit down. I'd like to talk to you."

I had never seen or spoken to a General before, much less ever been invited into his office, so to say I was nervous was an understatement. And the crack about the long hair was certainly not a big help. I did know one thing about Generals though, when they say 'come on in', you come on in.

"Shut the door, would you." He said.

This looks like trouble, when they say to 'shut the door', it means that they are about to ream you out. So I shut the door and sat where he told me to sit. I kept silent and decided to let him talk and try not to act stupid. Sometimes that's hard for me to do.

The first thing out of his mouth was disarming.

"You're McAllister aren't you? Well, what do you think of Wichita?"

Fortunately that was a rhetorical question because he didn't wait for an answer and I kept silent.

"I understand you're prior service. Have you thought about coming into the Reserves? Why don't you see Sergeant Dodson? What are you planning to do with this team? When are you going to get a haircut? We have a drill every Monday from six to ten pm and the staff meets down the hall in Mr. Hall's office, you should be there. The tenant units drill on the weekends. You should meet some of our people. By the way, there will be a Warrant vacancy available soon, would you like me to put your name in for it?"

I stood there with my mouth hanging open and nodded my head.

"Should I take that as a 'yes'?" He said and smiled broadly.

What a night!

I've been here a week, it was five degrees below zero when I got up this morning and there was six inches of snow on the ground, and last night I had a Brigadier General tell me that I needed a haircut and that I'm expected to attend their staff meetings. This doesn't look like the smartest thing I ever did in my life.

Before I go on, I should explain what the General meant when he said something about a "Warrant". In the enlisted ranks, there are several grades of Sergeants. They are called 'Non-Commissioned Officers' or NCO's. In the Officer corps, there are Commissioned Officers ranging from Second Lieutenant to General. In between is a small group of four grades of Warrant Officers. Usually they are the shop chiefs and supervisors of the various areas.

It was so cold that my car barely turned over, but it proved its worth when it fired to life. It's a good thing I bought a new battery for the car before I left home. I gave twenty three hundred dollars for the Porsche from my high school friend, Ted Collins, at Phil Winslow VW back home in the Springs. It was a demo with forty five hundred miles on it. You don't get this kind of really special deal from a car dealer very often so I take extra special care of this little beauty.

The snow is really heavy and wet and I'm plowing the first tracks through it in the streets. I had breakfast at that little café the guy at the 'Y' told me about and the place was nearly empty. The clock on the wall was just striking seven o'clock when I left the café to get to the office. With the snow and cold and the street lights that didn't work, it took me twenty five minutes to drive the fifteen or twenty blocks to get there.

Oh, great! There's no one here to open the doors to the building, not one car in the parking lot. Well, I'll go around back and see the shop foreman. I've been told that he always had a smile on his face and is always pretty friendly. Good, he's there!

"Hi. You're the shop foreman? I'm DJ McAllister. I'm on the MAIT team." I said.

He stuck out his hand to me.

"Hi DJ. You can call me 'Dusty'. Nice to meet you, I've already heard about the long hair. You've really got the staff talking. They can't figure you out, and Sixth Army didn't provide much guidance for the team they were putting in here. What's MAIT anyway?" He said.

"Maintenance Assistance and Instruction Team. Don't you just love it?" I said.

"Yeah! Army loves to name everything, don't they?" He said.

"Actually, your hair isn't too long, it's just that some of these guys are pretty straight laced here, especially the Colonels." He said. "It'll get better after you're here for a while."

"It was General Masters that said something about my hair."

"Oh, oh! Tough to beat the General. You know what you have to do now." He said.

"Yeah! Yeah! I know."

He said that he could see the parking lot from his office, so we got our coffee and sat down there. Ten minutes later we could see a little white VW that was made into a Baja bug with huge tires in the back throwing snow like a motorboat on water. I started to get up and go outside, but Dusty motioned for me to sit.

"Take it easy, that's only Gene Di Angelo, he'll make it in to work with that thing he's driving even if we have ten feet of snow." He said.

The snow stopped flying and there was a person coming toward us out of the snow cloud.

The cloud guy came to the door and shook off all the snow and entered the office.

"Hey Gene, meet DJ McAllister. He's part of that new team up front." Dusty said.

Gene and I went through the introductions and told each other our life stories. Gene is Gino Di Angelo. Same age as I am, five feet nine, a hundred sixty five pounds, muscular, curly brown hair, brown eyes, presently in the active Army Reserves as a Staff Sergeant in DCSLOG and he always seems to be smiling.

His specialties are all vehicles and special purpose equipment. He is a welder and a car nut, single and most of all according to Dusty, all the girls love him. Really love him. And he makes the most of it. He told us about his 'latest' while we had our coffee.

It's no wonder the girls like him, he has a smooth voice and looks as strong as an ox.

"I went to a trade school when I got out of high school for welding, auto body repair, internal combustion engine repair and stumbled onto this job. Been working for the Reserves ever since." He said.

In the winter, when it gets cold here, it really gets cold. It was cold and damp for the first part of the week. Thursday the sun came out and melted some of the snow so I went down the street a few blocks to a barber to get a haircut, and wouldn't you know, the first thing out of the barber's mouth was a smart remark.

"Oh, you're the one with the long hair. Ha, ha, ha. I've been expecting you." He said. "I hear the General really got on you. That's okay, I'll cut it so he'll like it."

I'll bet he's in the unit there and heard about it the same night. He's probably been counting his money ever since he first heard.

"Wait a minute!" I said. "What about me? How about if you cut it so I'll like it?"

Oh K a a a y." He said. "Maybe I can give you a compromise between you and the General."

I came out looking like I did when I was in the service several years ago, white sidewalls and everything. At least I'll be able to go to the staff meeting on Monday. I have got to find a good non-military barber right away, maybe a woman.

The following Monday was as uneventful as all the other days had been. After supper, I arrived at the Arcom for the staff meeting, where I was introduced to all the G staff and the aides by General Masters. There was some talk about long hair, but nothing definite and no finger pointing.

The man in charge here is a two star Major General named Johnson. The meeting went well. I sat in a corner and kept my mouth shut. After the meeting was over, they all said how glad they were to meet me and have me, and eventually the team, here. Boy, what a load of bull.

The second man on the team arrived Monday February 12. Interesting guy. Rodney Hill, forty four, retired Master Sergeant, short, stocky, built like a fireplug, came down from Fort Riley where he was in vehicle maintenance. He had a letter introducing him and saying that he would be interim team chief until the fourth man comes.

"You're McAllister?" He said. "I'm Rodney Hill. You can call me Rod. They tell you anything?"

"Not much." I said. "I go by DJ."

"Well, DJ, I guess we'll just do it our way until somebody says something." He said. "Let's see if we can get an office of our own."

The next day we were moving into a tiny office just a little bigger than a closet down at the end of the hall, but it was all ours, until someone finds out about it, that is. The following day we got a phone! No telling where he picked that up.

The day after that we got three desks and a big metal locker for supplies. He said they were excess and stored out in back. I could see why they made him interim team chief, he just got things started right away. I'll bet he has some history in supply, because he is an experienced scrounger.

A week later the third man on the team arrived. Gary Andersson, fifty seven, First Sergeant, Mess Steward and cook, tall, thin with a paunch and bald. He worked for the South Dakota National Guard as their Division Mess Steward and full-time cook.

After the introductions, we sat down and tried to make up a schedule of what we thought needed to be done. The next day Rod called Sixth Army for some information about our job here. Rod was on the phone for an hour or more and made at least five phone calls.

"He said we don't work for them." Rod said.

"What the hell does that mean?" I said.

"The best that I can understand of what that Colonel out there told me is that the Readiness Regions took over command and control of all the teams two weeks ago. So I guess I'll call Denver and try to find out something from them." Rod said.

Rod got on the phone to Readiness Region VIII in Denver, and after half a dozen more phone calls he finally got something.

"Well it's true. We work for the Region and we're called MAIT 23. It stands for Maintenance Assistance and Instruction Team, but we already knew that. You feel like an assistant or an instructor? I'll bet there's a kink somewhere in the works that we don't know about yet." Rod said.

"Some Colonel at the Region told me to have the Captain call him when he got into the office. I didn't even know we were getting a Captain." He said.

During the next two weeks, we got our team on the publications account, stole a couple more phones and a blackboard and went over to the NCO club on the Air Force base and got ourselves some membership cards for the club.

Each of us wrote down what we thought our qualifications and specialties were, and tried to get to know each other and as many of the full-time reserve people as we could. If we are going to be in their building, we might as well be friends.

It looks to me like the best friend I could find in that whole area is going to be Dusty Rhodes. We talk alike, we like the same things and he seems to know what I'm thinking before I do. Dusty is a Chief Warrant in charge of the shop during drills and a WS-9 in charge of the shop during the day. He has been in the reserves for a long time from what I can figure. Besides, he's several years older than I am.

Here it is the first of April and we were just notified that the Captain will be reporting into the office on Monday. This ought to be interesting.

Region Eight sent us a fact sheet on him last month which all three of us read with great interest. Rod read it and took some notes and passed it around to Gary and I. Captain Caleb Burton, thirty, Infantry, last assignment Fort Benning. They assigned a grunt to do logistics inspections.

Monday morning, at about eight thirty, pardon me, that's 0830 in Army talk, the Captain made his grand entrance. He's dressed in khakis and you could cut your finger on the crease in his shirt. We introduced ourselves all around and he said to call him Burt. I checked his brass when he walked in and sure enough, crossed rifles.

We all sat around and had a head session about what had been going on at Region and here in the Arcom.

"By the way, you need to call that Colonel at Region." Rod said.

"What do you guys do for lunch around here?" The Captain asked.

He acted like he didn't hear what Rod said.

"How about the O Club?" He asked.

"What do you mean O Club, we're Sergeants." Gary said.

"Not any more. You're GS-9's now, and that makes you officers." Burt said.

So off to the Officers Club we went. Burt picked up three membership forms at the office for us to fill out for the O Club.

We found a table in the corner and took a seat and the waitress brought our orders. As soon as the waitress left, around behind Gary walked this unbelievably, fantastically gorgeous woman dressed in a very skimpy outfit. I'm not kidding. I was facing Gary and I took it all in.

"Hi boys, how's everything? Can I get you anything?" She whispered.

Well, I chocked on my hamburger and about fell off my chair doing it. Rod's eyes popped out onto the floor, and poor Gary didn't even see her. Probably didn't hear her either. She was standing right behind him. He must be deaf, or thick.

"This is my wife, Gwen." Burt said.

Neither Rod nor I can talk and Gary acted like he didn't know what was going on. I'll bet he really didn't. Finally Rod chocked out something.

"It looks like we better be getting back to the office." He said as he stood up. I took my hamburger and followed Rod.

Back at the office the Captain told us that he and his wife set up that little scene as a joke, and it worked. We bit on it big time.

The Captain called this Colonel at the Region and after about forty minutes on the phone he said that we would be doing classes for the National Guard and the Army Reserve units in southern and western Kansas. And we would be expected to go out to the units and drum up business.

"The Colonel told me to find out what they do and make up some classes to help them with their readiness." Burt said.

"We have over a hundred Reserve units in this Arcom and I don't know how many Guard units there are here in this area, so we'll have to split up." Rod said.

I was assigned Commo, electronics, CBR and small arms. I had a gun shop with a friend a few years ago back in the Springs so I guess that makes me qualified.

I still have several weapons at home. One in particular is my favorite. A nine millimeter semi automatic with a silencer and a shoulder holster. I call it 'James Bond', because that's the one he uses in the movies. I have a permit for it back there, but I left it home for now. I have to get info on their regs about guns in this state.

Rod is assigned all vehicles and special purpose equipment. Gary will do all food service equipment and help with the special purpose equipment and small arms.

The Captain will do all the records and the rest of the equipment. The team will go to Denver for a conference at the Region Headquarters in December. But right now it is April and we need to get started.

Rod and I went to Fort Riley and checked out an aging Chevrolet four door sedan all painted up in that adorable olive drab green color with white letters on the door that tells everyone the company that owns the car. The Captain and Gary got a car with the same color scheme from the Arcom. So we set out to visit some of the units, Rod and I went west, and Gary and Burt went east. This should be nothing but fun.

Chapter 3

Getting Started

Civilians that work for the Army Reserve units are called Administrative and Supply Technicians (AST). These people work full time forty hours a week in the office where they coordinate the affairs of the unit on a daily basis. During the drills they could do various other jobs. The AST could be the First Sergeant, The Commander or any other person in a key position in the unit. For our team's purposes, they are our contacts in the unit.

April was a pretty slow month. It's the start of spring and its warming to a decent temperature. Rod and I visited all the units on the west side of town on Monday. On Tuesday we drove to Kingman, the next town west on Highway 54, and Pratt, the next after that.

The AST's in the National Guard units were not interested in what we had to say and made no effort to disguise it. Their attitude was, "Go away boy, you bother me!" At least the USAR units knew they had problems. They didn't want our help, but they knew they had problems.

From Pratt you take US 281 due north to Great Bend where we got the same reception from the units there. From there we decided to go over to the interstate and hit McPherson and Newton on the way

back. Same kind of attitude as before. We spent a
week driving around the back roads of Kansas, visited twelve units and had all twelve tell us the same
thing. "Get out of our life!" This looks like it's really
gonna be fun.

The following Monday we all talked about what
to do about the problems we had. Gary and the
Captain encountered the same things as we did. The
Captain got on the phone and the rest of us had a
brainstorming session. We came up with some ideas
that might work. The Captain said he would take
care of it, after all, that is his job.

I have been at the "Y" for five months now and it
seemed like a good idea to get my own place. With
all the money I'm making now, I can afford a cheap
house here to throw my stuff in. I was talking to one
of the AST's about getting a place of my own when
he gave me a business card.

"Here, call her, she's good and she gives special
service for first time buyers, and be sure to mention
my name. He said.

OK. So what could I lose by calling a referral like
this? I went back to the office and got on the phone
and made the call to Stewart Realty.

"Hello. Stewart Realty, Mary Ellen speaking."
Her voice was pleasant and cheerful.

"Hi. This is DJ McAllister. I was given your card
by Sergeant Williams, and I'm looking for a house."

I made an appointment to meet her at her office
to go over what kind of house I wanted. Pretty standard stuff. We talked for about half an hour after I

arrived and she suggested that we go look at a couple of places. When we went out to get into her car, she flipped me the keys.

"Here, you drive." She said.

Her office was on the west side of the river on Harry Street, and soon we were on our way to look at a couple of houses on Laura and Lulu Streets. I'm not familiar with these street names.

We were only a block away from her office when she tickled my ear with her finger. That took me by surprise and I almost ran up on the curb. I'm supposed to be looking for a street and an address, in a town I've only been living in for five months. And she's tickling me. I can barely see the road! Good, here's a red light. A good time to stop.

At least she stopped what she was doing at the light.

Now the lights green, and the guy behind me is blowing his horn. I'm going to go to the first side street I see and turn off. Look at that! It's the street we were looking for anyway. I'll try to keep my composure and go down the street till I see a Real Estate sign. I pulled over in front of the house and stopped.

"Wow! What was that all about?"

She fluffed her hair like nothing had happened.

"I have a special service that I provide to men that are first time buyers. I thought it would calm you down and then you could look at the house with a clear head." She said.

"Calm me down? I'm always calm, but now I am a little jittery after that surprise."

"Every time we go out to look at houses, I'll provide a special service, and after you close on one I'll make love to you in your new house, but that will be the last time you see me." She said.

"It's only for first time buyers?" I must have sounded like the kid that just rode in on the turnip truck.

"Yes. I'm good at what I do and I like what I'm doing and I get an awful lot of referrals. Last year I sold thirty-eight houses and my associate sold thirty. She takes longer than I do." She said.

We would have gone in to look at the house where I stopped, but it was the wrong house. I drove shakily two more blocks down the street and parked in front of the house with the right sign in the yard and went in. I felt rubbery in the knees, but after a few minutes of walking I began to return to normal.

"Did she say, every time?"

It looks like we might be looking at houses for quite a while. I smiled for a long time about that idea while we inspected the house.

The next day I told the other guys about our neighborhood real estate agent and her friendly service and it looks like she'll sell three more houses soon.

The team went out on a trip the next week to Salina to visit the 123rd Truck Company. The vehicles and small arms are in sad shape and so are the records. We gave what suggestions we could, but I got the feeling that's as far as it'll go.

After two days in Salina, I was ready, ready hell, I was in a hurry to get back to town and see another house with that special service. I had told her about my unusual schedule and to be expecting a call from the other guys on the team. I wasn't in the office two minutes till I made the call to set up the next meeting.

She answered the phone with her usual salutation.

"Hello. Stewart Realty, Mary Ellen speaking."

"Hi. It's DJ."

"Hi there! The other three men on your team called and I'm going to try to set up appointments with them." She said. "When do you want to look at another house with me?"

After stammering for a while, I said to make it as soon as possible, which she did.

The next three or four houses might as well have been on the moon, because I don't remember a thing except the service. What a wonderful service.

The following Monday, all four of us piled into our pretty green Chevy and headed for Garden City, it's two hundred forty miles. By the time we were leaving Pratt, it was starting to warm up. According to Rod, May is one of the pleasant months in Kansas, so we better make the most of it.

Garden City was basking in eighty degree temperature as we parked in the motel parking lot.

As my regular 'in the office' duty, I'm supposed to set up motel reservations and cars. 'Whatever has to do with travel' is the way the Captain put it. I made the reservations at a motel I had never heard of in a town I had never heard of. We'll be staying at the Wheatland Motel and go to the unit in the morning.

After a good breakfast in the coffee shop, we drove to the unit. It's in a strip of stores and their place can't be twenty feet across. The AST, Jim Bulger, met us at the door and was so cheerful and bubbly that I thought there was something wrong with him. It was seven thirty in the morning. You're not supposed to be like that at this time of day.

"Good Morning, gents. Lovely day isn't it? Can I get you some coffee?" He said.

Rod grumbled and I mumbled something.

"Sure, I'll have some." Gary said.

Jim poured coffee for all of us and turned his attention to Burt. The Captain sat down to brief him about what we planned to do here today.

The four of us decided last week that the best way to help these units was to inspect their equipment and records and tell them what we found so that we could start some kind of instruction classes. We all went to look at the equipment with a pad and a pencil. You wouldn't believe it. They are using those old PRC-6 and PRC-10 radios as commo gear. It was old stuff when I was in.

"Hey Jim, let's get into the vault and look at the weapons." I said.

Jim let Gary and I into the vault to start with the M-16s. The first one I picked up, I pulled the charger back and it had the bolt in it. The bolts are supposed to be stored separately in a safe. Besides that, it wasn't cleaned after it was used last. It looked like someone painted the insides with black paint, then dumped in some dirt on top of the paint.

"Hey Jim, when did the Troop use the weapons last?" I asked.

"Well let's see." He said as he went through the records. "They went to Fort Riley to use the range back in November, I think."

Gary has one just like it in his hands. He began to smile.

"I think I'm going to like this inspection stuff a little." Gary said as his grin widened.

Rod looked at their one Jeep and the one M-113 and said they were in sad shape too. But the Captain came back and said the records were perfect. So it's pretty obvious to everyone that the AST is doing his job, but the guys in the unit are not.

About that time the Commander came in, a young Captain in jeans. Burt took this young Captain back to his office and closed the door to give him the news about his unit. We decided to go down the street to the VFW for a sandwich. It would probably be a while, Burt had a good head of steam built up.

The next day we went on to the next Troop in the Squadron located in Scott City. In western Kansas, Nebraska and eastern Colorado, there are a lot of little towns that are there solely because of the farming and ranching that goes on in these areas. Most all of these towns have a population of a hundred to a thousand folks with a gas station, restaurant, church, maybe a motel and sometimes a theater. Scott City fits the description except the population is about three thousand.

When we got to the unit in Scott City, we found Jim waiting for us. His same cheerful self. We had coffee and he showed us where everything was stored.

I was looking at the Publications Account when I heard Rod chuckling across the room. He motioned to me.

"C'mere, look at this." He said. "This is their Mobilization Plan", (MobPlan for short). "It should say where they go when the Troop is mobilized in case of war. Listen to this. They say that the Commander, his driver and a radio operator will ride in their one and only Jeep with their one and only radio. Following closely behind, the rest of the Troop will be riding in their only other vehicle, an M-113. But that isn't the best part. They are going to drive to Fort Hood. Texas! On the state and local roads!" By this time, Rod was laughing out loud.

Just to explain. An M-113 is a tracked vehicle called an APC, which is used to haul a dozen or so troops across the rough terrain. It has a ramp at the rear for fast loading and unloading and is driven with two vertical handles, joysticks, on each side of the driver that control track speed and direction. It has the ability to turn on a dime by pulling one stick back and pushing the other forward. This maneuver, however, leaves a nice round hole, a donut, in the ground. One big thing about the 113 is that it is made of thick aluminum and when the sun comes up, it gets hot, really hot.

He began to laugh, and the more I thought of it, I started to laugh too.

"Can't you just see it? A jeep and a track driving down a hot asphalt highway in July or August, ripping it up as they go, and all the guys sweating to death in that big aluminum tin can? It's so ridiculous that it's funny!" He said. "You know what the best part of this whole thing is? There's a Santa Fe freight station not five blocks away." He pointed in the direction of the station.

At about that time, Jim walked in with the commander of the Troop. He is a young Lieutenant, and Jim introduced him all around. Rod began to laugh and I couldn't help myself, I did too.

We found the Troop here in the same shape as the other one. But we could tell that no one from the higher headquarters had ever been here in an advisory capacity.

During the out briefing, we explained how the track should be shipped and what the Mob Plan should say. Tomorrow we'll go to Great Bend where the Squadron Headquarters and one of the Troops are located.

Great Bend, Kansas is a pretty good sized town for the area it is in. The main industries are farming, the Fuller Brush Company, and the Santa Fe railroad. In the morning we found a nice little café on Main Street, so we had two eggs, hash browns, toast and coffee for a dollar and a quarter. Good breakfast, unbelievable price!

By the time we walked in to the USAR center, word had already come from the other Troops about

what we found and there was a reception commit-
tee at the door. The Squadron Commander, a Major,
jumped the Captain right away. The rest of us just
went over with our briefcases and sat down out of
the line of fire.

"Who the hell do you think you are? Pulling an
inspection on my people! What gives you the right to
tell my Troop commanders that they aren't qualified
to do their job?" The Major screamed.

"If you will call Colonel Lewis at the Arcom, you
will find that he and I and the General discussed this
same problem before we ever left Wichita. They will
back us one hundred percent." The Captain said.

"Major, if this Troop and the headquarters here
are as bad as the other Troops that we looked at, you
will certainly be explaining why you did not pull the
inspections on your people yourself, instead of waiting for someone from the outside like us to do it,"
Burt said.

Burt was enjoying this and a little smile began to
curl one lip.

"You can't blame it on anyone else like you've been
trying to do, since we found the records in Garden
City and Scott City to be in perfect condition. This
problem is certainly a command problem, and I am
laying it on your doorstep!"

Burt tried to hide his smile and amusement earlier,
but no longer. He was beaming from ear to ear, but
the Major was scowling.

"Now if you will show me where my team and I
can work, we will get started with these units. We

will need desks and access to all of your records and equipment. And we need to get into the vault too." Burt said.

I really think Burt enjoyed that a little too much. He unloaded on that Major like a first grade teacher with a troublesome kid.

We went through those units like a dose of salts and by the time it was time for lunch, we had written so much that all of our hands hurt from cramps.

The AST asked if we wanted to go somewhere special for lunch, so he took us to The Wallace Buffet. What a treat! All you can eat for three and a quarter. So we did.

During lunch, the AST said that the unit had been this way for a long time and the Commander had been trying to put the blame on him for the whole time.

"We know. Jim Bulger already filled us in on the Major's comments." Burt said.

When we got back from lunch, you could see that the Major was not happy. It seems the he called the Arcom and was told to cooperate with the team. And since there were questions about the Squadrons capability and his performance as a commander, he finally got the message that his career in the USAR might be short-lived.

We decided to sit down and write as much as possible while the loud discussions between the Major and Burt were going on. After an hour of this, Rod went over and butted in and said that we would have to go back to the motel to write since there was so much noise here. We wrote all afternoon and put the report together so that we could brief it in the morning.

As planned, we went in to the Reserve center in the morning to brief our findings to the AST and the Major. Colonel Lewis had driven up from Wichita to hear the out briefing. The Captain and the Colonel had a short meeting behind closed doors before Burt got started. The Colonel was seated in the most advantageous spot for him to see the reactions of all the people.

The Major was furious that we would dare say that his Squadron and the subordinate Troops were not equal to Army standards for readiness. But the Colonel and the Major had a meeting after it was all over and by the look on his face, it really was all over.

The trip from Great Bend back to Wichita was an interesting one. The Captain decided that we should drive back through Sterling and Hutchinson and a bunch of other little towns along the river. By the time we got to Hutch, he was finished with the little towns and Rod took over and drove to the interstate and flew in on that. It only took us twice as long as normal.

The next day while we were in the office, Mr. Gibson came up and asked a lot of questions about the Squadron. A week later at the staff meeting, the Captain found out that the Major had been relieved.

During the rest of the month, Gary and Burt bought a house and Rod had one under contract.

It looks like the team is finally getting settled in. Of course I had to see a house or two just to stay in touch.

June in Kansas is a wet month. Back home, we had a daily rain in Colorado Springs in the early afternoon about two o'clock and it lasted about fifteen or twenty minutes. Those rains were nothing compared to the rains they get here.

In the spring, the storms come whether you want them or not. Our first encounter with these surprises was the eighth of June. It was a beautiful beginning of the day when I drove to the office today. We were in the office at the regular time, seven thirty. At about eight thirty the rain started and by ten it was becoming dark. By eleven thirty it was as dark as night outside with thunder and lightning and high winds sounding like the building was going to come down around us at any minute.

We all got up and went to the windows to see what was going on outside. The sky was dark and it was like night time at noon. I have never seen anything like this before anywhere I have been in this country. And I've been around.

Soon there were bright flashes of lightning followed by extra loud rumbles of thunder. I know what that is, but here in Kansas and Missouri, it means danger with a capital D. The banging continued for at least an hour before it began to subside. There were a few extremely loud bangs that sounded very close, and sent several folks running for the basement.

I wanted to see what this whole thing was all about, so I stayed upstairs so I could see. We don't see this kind of thing in the Rockies. There was a TV set in the school's office, so I ran down there. There were a lot of maps shown and the weatherman was explaining what was happening. Then a cameraman showed a funnel cloud drop out of a cloud and he explained where it was seen. Anywhere in the state is too close for me.

The locals acted like it was nothing. But to four guys with no prior knowledge of these events, it became a little scary. We heard on the radio that a tornado touched down about twenty miles out of town to the east. That's too close for me! I'm ready to go home.

Chapter 4

Fredonia

The trip through the southeast part of Kansas has to be the best trip we have ever taken. Not because the weather has finally become warm enough that we didn't need those heavy coats and sweaters. Not because of the units we visited, but that was good. Not because of the girl I met, but that was better. But the best part can be filed under our esteemed Captain, Burt.

The plan was to visit the Transportation Company located in Independence, Parsons and Pittsburg. A relatively short trip through the back roads and small towns, which should have been uneventful.

We left around eight am Monday morning, and the Captain said he wanted to drive the first leg. I decided to get in the back seat and hunker down in the corner. From Wichita you take Kansas route 96 ninety three miles to Fredonia, then route 47 three miles to US 75 and twenty five miles to Independence. Rod rode shotgun with the map and was acting as navigator.

Everything was going great, even though it was starting to get hot outside, and inside. We should be able to make our first stop by noon. As we entered Fredonia, Rod said, "Whoa, the speed limit just dropped to thirty, better slow down." The car was only going about forty at the time.

Burt put his foot on the brake and got it down in a hurry and we crept through town at a snail's pace.

Somewhere around the center of town, we saw a flashing light and Burt said, "Looks like an ambulance coming, I better pull over." So he did. But the lights didn't go on past us, they stopped right behind us.

"Oh, oh. This isn't good." I said.

The Officer got out of his car and walked up to the driver's door.

"Drivers license and registration, please." He said sounding a little surly.

"What seems to be the problem, Officer?" Burt asked.

"You know how fast you were goin'?" Asked the Officer.

"Why, yes I do. Exactly thirty miles per hour." Burt said.

"I got you on radar at thirty-one, and that's a punishable offense." He said.

Each time the Officer spoke, his voice got louder and more brusque. And each time Burt spoke back, he was the same. Here it comes!

"THIRTY-ONE? That's outrageous! Unbelievable! Ridiculous!" Burt shouted each word louder than the last.

Burt was going on and on again.

"Who are you anyway, all dressed up in some kind of funny uniform?" He said.

We got trouble now! The Officer just called Burt's uniform, 'funny'. Watch out for the fireworks.

Burt jumped out of the car and began to tell the Officer the he was in the presence of a United States

Army Captain, and that he did not wear a funny uniform.

"You're under arrest!" The Officer said. "And so are your accomplices! Let's go!"

We all got out onto the street so the Officer could search and handcuff us. He made a call for backup and soon another car arrived on the scene. We were all herded into the two police cars and transported to the local jail. I couldn't stop laughing and that irritated our police friends a lot.

"You'll laugh when you see the Judge in the morning!" He said.

That made me laugh even more.

It was a long night in that cold cell, but Burt kept us all warm and awake with his ranting. They did bring us some food along about five o'clock, and I laughed some more. Two pieces of dry white bread, sorry looking wilted lettuce and a piece of bologna, with lukewarm coffee in a tin cup. It's getting funnier by the minute.

The sun came up the next morning and shortly thereafter came the Super Cop.

"Let's go, you guys! It's time to go before the Judge!" He said loudly.

It didn't take long for us to be herded into the court room and be seated down in front.

"Next case." The Judge said.

The bailiff called the case and the Officer herded us through that little swinging door to the front.

"What's going on here, Officer Knorr?" The Judge asked.

"Your Honor, I caught these four desperate looking criminals on their way through our town to do

who-knows-what and I brought them in last night."
He said.

I had been standing on the end with my hands
cuffed behind my back and I decided to bend over
and move around to get my hands out in front where
they would be a little more comfortable.

The Judge noticed my movements and stopped
Super Cop in mid sentence and said, "You have these
people handcuffed in my court?"

"Yes Your Honor, they could be dangerous!" He
said.

"Bailiff, remove all the handcuffs and take Officer
Knorr over there to the side." He said and pointed to
where he wanted Super Cop to be standing.

"What are the charges?" The Judge asked.

"Speeding sir. I clocked them at thirty-one miles
per hour on Main Street." Knorr said.

"Thirty-one? What's the matter with you, Billy?
You've been doing this for a long time and it's time I
stopped it right now! Bailiff! Remove his badge and
weapon! Mary! Call the Chief and get him over here
right now!" The Judge banged his gavel so hard I
thought he would break it.

"Billy, you have been warned! Now I will make
this final! I am relieving you of duty as of right now!
You are no longer a police officer in this town, and if
I have anything to say about it, you will never be one
again! Anywhere! EVER!"

"I see you called for backup. Who did you call?"
He asked.

Officer Boyle came to my aid in the other car." Super Cop said with a noticeably shaky voice.

"Get him in here!" The Judge is really worked up now.

About that time the Chief walked in.

"Chief, I have removed Billy from your employ and now I am going to sentence him to six months in the city jail! And if he says one word I will double it!" He banged his gavel again so hard I thought it would break again. He was yelling now. It looks like Super Cop isn't so super any more.

The Judge addressed the Captain. He was visibly calmed down after all the yelling he did at Billy.

"Captain, tell me what you and your men were doing here yesterday."

Burt explained our mission and the reason for the trip today. He added a few colorful expletives when he told about the traffic stop in the late morning yesterday, their wonderful food, and the night in their jail. But he held himself in check very nicely during it all. I was surprised.

"You see what you've done Billy? These men work for the US Army and you are treating them like common criminals. That is the reason you have been removed from the job, and you can think about that while you examine that jail cell you seem to love to put people in. Case dismissed! Sorry for the trouble Captain. I hope you won't hold it against us." The Judge said.

When we found the car, Rod slid behind the wheel and we were off again. The drive to Independence wasn't bad, about thirty miles down US 75 and we were there. We drove straight to the unit and in a couple of hours, we were done. Everything looked pretty good here. One thing did come up though, the AST asked why we didn't arrive yesterday. He said that's what he was told.

"Fredonia!" Rod said.

They all laughed about that and he said that he forgot to warn us about that. Rod explained that there won't be any more trouble in Fredonia now. They all said that they were glad about that.

"Well, since you're already late, why don't you go through Coffeeville on the way to Parsons? Coffee-ville has quite a history, you know. It's nice to see some of it close up and it's only about thirty miles out of the way. Take 160 seven miles to 169 then twenty miles to Coffeeville. See you in Parsons." He said.

"You know, maybe we could use a little diversion after that fiasco in Fredonia." Burt said. "Let's go to Coffeeville."

Rod drove the twenty seven miles and found a nice little café for lunch. I have always wanted to go to Coffeeville. Stories of the old west are full of tales of outlaws, lawmen, robberies and shoot-outs in and around Coffeeville, and the opportunity to actually see this town is going to be a real treat.

I expected Coffeeville to be a lot like Dodge City. Dodge has a string of old buildings set up along Front Street to look like a town of the 1870's, with a Santa Fe steam engine at the depot and a museum or two with really interesting mementos of the old west and other things to see. We spent half a day on Front Street when we visited Dodge. Coffeeville didn't have any of that.

We decided to spend the night there and go to Parsons bright and early in the morning.

The trip from Coffeeville was along back roads and took more time than any of us expected but we arrived in Parsons before noon and I found the motel I had staked out.

Parsons has another unit of the same Company and an Army Maintenance and Supply Activity (AMSA). We went directly to the unit and met the AST and the rest of the men. After a brief tour of the unit and the AMSA, we went to the motel to check in and get some lunch. I had seen a little burger stand down the block, so I excused myself and walked out for some fresh air and a quick bite.

I walked around town with my burger and drink until I found a park bench to sit on. Directly in front of me was another bench with a beautiful brown haired girl dressed in jeans and a white shirt sitting there watching me and eating her burger and drink.

"Hi." I said.

"Hi, yourself. You're not from around here, are you?" She asked.

"No. Here on business. My name is DJ."

"That's not a name. Those are initials." She said.

"Sorry, best I can do."

"What kind of work do you do?" She asked.

"I work for the Government."

"My name is Louise, and I work at the bank." She pointed across the street to the bank.

"Well Louise, I've finished my burger and I have to get to work, but could I have dinner with you tonight after we get off work?"

"Well, I don't usually go out with a guy I've only known for a few minutes, but I'll take a chance on you." She said and she laughed a little.

"Now comes the hard part. I'm traveling with three other guys and they will want to use our car. Can you come and get me?"

She said she would and I told her the motel and the room that I was in. She arrived at five thirty and was dressed to kill. She's about five foot nine, maybe six foot in heels. We went to a restaurant she knew in the center of town that had the best steaks. After the meal we walked around town and talked. We arrived back at the motel about seven thirty.

"Would you like to come in?" I asked.

"Maybe just for a minute." She said.

The phone rang at six am and I picked it up. "Your wake up call." Someone said and hung up.

I was already awake and so was she. "Well, it looks like it's time to shower and go to work again." I said.

"Yes, but I'm going to feel a lot better at work to-day. Thanks for everything, and the next time you're in Parsons, you have my number." She said.

Louise and I were already having breakfast when the guys strolled into the coffee shop. We did our greetings, finished eating and left for Pittsburg. Rod and Gary were smiling a lot.

Gary drove the next leg to Pittsburg. Another forty miles along highway 160, then highway 69 to Pittsburg. Just try to find your way back!

"Where we stayin' DJ?" He said.

"The Holiday Inn."

"Pretty fancy." He said.

"Maybe, but it was the best price in town."

"Let's find the Reserve Center and do the introductions. Then we can get checked in and come back after lunch." Burt said.

Burt really has a way with words. We've been doing this for how long? And he has to tell us every little detail. So, on to the Reserve Center, meet and greet, back to the motel, check in, unpack, lunch, and ready to go to work.

Even though we had the Headquarters Company and A Company to do, it went very quickly. We were done by four o'clock. We'll write tonight and out brief in the morning and go.

"What are you guys doing tonight?" The AST asked. "You ever been to Chicken Mary's?"

We all looked at each other with that silly look you get after a question like that. Sergeant Josephson had his answer. It looks like we won't get much writing done tonight

Chicken Mary's is a restaurant and bar in the middle of nowhere in the woods east of town. They serve the best chicken I can remember with all the fixin's. A fine bar, and the prices were reasonable, but it's really hard to find if you don't know. And we didn't.

The trip last night set everything back hours. We'll be lucky to get this finished and briefed today. We pulled out at two fifteen and headed for Wichita. Three little units and we had to drive all over the country and it took a whole week.

The Captain decided that he would drive straight through. And not through Fredonia. We arrived at the office well after dark. I have got to get some sleep.

In late June I finally found a house that was too good to pass up. The house is an old frame bungalow built in the twenties on Pattie Street with air conditioning and a basement.

It looks like it was built with a crawl space and later was dug out since the inside basement walls were in from the concrete walls for the house with a shelf of about four feet and the basement floor isn't anywhere near level. A big living room with a fireplace and two middle sized bedrooms. It also has a two car garage off the alley in the back. Like I said, for fifteen thousand three hundred it was too good to pass up.

During the next two or three weeks, I was shopping at all the used furniture and second hand stores for things to furnish this place with. Actually I did pretty well. The biggest expense was the wall to wall carpeting in the living room. That had to be removed and replaced before any furniture could be put in.

The house is shaping up pretty well and it's Friday night, I think I'll kick back tonight. I normally get off about four in the afternoon, so I picked up a case of Pepsi on the way home.

Tonight there is a baseball game on TV, and I have plenty of food and drink. What could be better? Little did I know.

At about six there was a knock at the door and I looked out to see a nice new shiny blue Cadillac parked at the curb. Before the second knock, I was at the door opening it to see my beautiful friend Mary Ellen standing there with a big smile on her face.

"Hi, I wanted to see what you had done with the place, and since I was in the neighborhood, here I am." She said.

"Come on in."

"I brought my curler case with me." She said.

Needless to say, I didn't watch the baseball game that night. That was the last time I ever saw Mary Ellen again.

Chapter 5

What's In A Name?

From the Roman Legions of centuries ago to the armies of today, any military service must be organized in order to operate properly. Commanders, whether they are commanding a war like Eisenhower did in the nineteen forties or a First Lieutenant commanding a tiny troop of infantrymen today, want everything identified.

Everything must be tied into a nice neat package, it must be sliced and diced, packed and stacked. And loggies are the ones who do it.

Logistics is the science of providing and maintaining personnel, equipment and supplies for day to day operations. The Army says it a different way. Servicing the Army in the field. Modern armies with complex new weapon systems and equipment require a huge logistical effort to put them into battle and keep them there.

This effort is sometimes called the 'Logistics Tail' and no one likes that Tail less than the commanders, especially the Generals. Logistics has a tendency to get in the way when you're fighting a war, but you can't win one without it. Sometimes I think this is the exact reason why inspectors were invented, to see that everything is in its place and coming along as it should.

Lastly, there is always a requirement to report the findings to those very same commanders who professed their dislike for the logistics community in the first place.

I can't believe that I was insane enough to leave Colorado Springs to work in Wichita. It's only May and the temperature is hovering in the nineties already.

But the good part of the story is that I get to travel the great American West. This is the place that inspired hundreds of novels by the most famous of authors and movies with the most famous named stars of the silver screen.

The American West is now considered the area between the Pacific Ocean and the Rocky Mountains. But during the time of the settling of this country, it extended to the Mississippi River with cowboys, Indians, outlaws, ghost towns and gold mines. Gold?

The great west borders the ocean, and encompasses the mountains and rivers, desert and forests, farms where wheat and many other vegetables to feed the country grow and great ranches where livestock are grown. There are very large cities down to tiny towns so small that you will not find a restaurant or a motel to stay the night.

Our area is the fifteen western states counting from the eastern border of Kansas to the ocean. I am looking forward to seeing these sights close up.

Each state has something different to give, some good and some not so good. North Dakota is cold,

Arizona is hot and dry, Washington is wet and Kansas is stormy, but each have positive attributes.

The great plains include Kansas, Nebraska, North and South Dakota. This prairie from Kansas to the Canadian border has hot summers, cold winters and moderate snowfall with summer temperatures reaching well over one hundred degrees. And the twenty to thirty five inches of rain promotes a vast ocean of wheat, corn and beans that could only grow there.

The Rocky Mountains stretch from far into Canada to just as far into Mexico. The dry cool weather seems ideal for livestock and vast forests of every kind of conifers which are ideal for building houses. There was a bonus of gold and silver found in these mountains a century ago.

The canyons and mesas of Utah with their unusual formations and stories of outlaw hideouts attached. The great northwest of Washington and Oregon support not only huge forests but even larger mountains. One, named Rainier, is the largest in the state.

The deserts of Nevada and Arizona have never been friendly to man, but the people who live on the fringes of heat and exhaustion are very friendly. I hope to see it all very soon.

It has always been the policy of armies and military leaders to attach names to campaigns, battles, objectives and areas of land for various reasons. During hostile actions, names were attached to invasions, reconnaissance, battles and maneuvers in order to identify and encode them. It's become a human habit, we type and identify everything by its name.

During Vietnam, there were hawks and doves and there was Operation Linebacker. During World War Two there was the Battle of the Bulge and during Korea there was the DMZ.

The Presidio of San Francisco was a Spanish fort built in 1776 on fifteen hundred acres at the point of land where the bay meets the Pacific Ocean. Fort Point was built at the southern point of the golden gate where the bridge is now standing. The Officer's Club was built in the same year and is now the oldest building in the city.

In that same Officer's Club, LTG Williams, the Commanding General of Sixth Army, was telling his Deputy Commander that he wanted his own inspection teams and he didn't want to wait to hire new people for these teams since there were already teams located within his purview.

We were told about the following meeting several months later by one of the guys on the San Francisco team.

"Let's transfer already established teams from somewhere. You have any ideas?" He asked his deputy.

"The Regions have teams, why not use theirs?" His Deputy said.

"Good! Assign the ones at the Arcom Headquarters and get them here for a conference to get things started." The General said. "Notify the Regions what we're doing and get the teams in here for a conference as soon as possible. I want them started right and soon."

"We're going to need a definitive name for these teams." The deputy said.

"That's something those loggies can do. Have them get a name and job description for these teams right away." He said to his Deputy.

The DCSLOG assigned Major Lockhart and Sergeant Collins to the task of finding an appropriate name for the General's new team of inspectors. The stakes are high and the time is short and there must be someone who can make something out of nothing.

After several days of brainstorming ideas for names and parts of the job description, only small parts were falling into place.

"We are in the logistics business. Maybe that should be in the name." Someone said.

"This is the headquarters, maybe command should be in the name." Another said.

"Yeah! We had CMMI, COMET, COLET, and other inspection teams over the past several years." Someone else said.

The room buzzed with activity for the next several hours with many ideas brought forth. Sometime after three on afternoon, while everyone's nose was to the grindstone, General Williams slipped into the room unnoticed and stood at the rear watching.

As a rule, Second Lieutenants aren't usually invited to participate in this kind of process. They are known to be impetuous and do not think things through before speaking. How Lieutenant Mangus found his way into this discussion no one knows. He sat against the wall for most of the day with his clipboard and pencil scribbling and every so often looking up when someone said something.

"I have it!" The young lieutenant sprang to his feet. "Command Logistics Inspection Team!"

"Sit down, Lieutenant! How would it sound for four of my toughest inspectors to walk into a MASH unit full of nurses and announce to the commander something like this? 'We are the CLIT team and we are here to examine your private parts.' The name I want for these teams should tell what they do, and nothing else." The General said.

"Maybe we should substitute Review for Inspection in the Lieutenants idea." A Major said.

General Williams walked to the front of the room.

"No thanks, Major, CLRT still sounds the same. Alright! I want the best ideas you have. I'll start with the First Sergeant."

The Sergeant rose to his feet with his tablet in hand.

"I kept coming back to one set of ideas, General. War Readiness Assistance Team. WRAT. The units always say we're a bunch of rats anyway, maybe now is the time for us to prove it." He said.

"I like it!" The General said.

"Now I want you to list exactly what they will inspect and the regs that govern not only the teams but the units as well. We will divide their mission into parts which can be inspected separately and graded.

Each will be combined with the others for a comprehensive total grade. A pass or fail scenario."

"Since each of the various areas of the units operation have their own regulations, the units should have them on hand and they should be cognizant of them. The teams must make sure the units have the regs and are trained in the correct use and maintenance of the equipment and the records associated with them." The General said.

It boiled down to this. We would inspect every piece of equipment the unit owned and every piece of paper associated with them and grade them with a pass or fail.

We would look at Food Service, Maintenance, Supply, Facilities and Safety, Mobilization, Security, Personnel Records and Plans and Publications.

The equipment would be lumped into general categories such as, Automotive, Special Purpose, Communications, CBR and Small Arms. The Army Maintenance Management System (TAMMS) would play a big role in the maintenance score.

I can only imagine how this will turn out. Not good for the units I'll bet.

Chapter 6

Getting Started ... Again

July brought a real surprise. All four of us had spent months trying to get this program up and running and now it looked like it was finally going to work. The phone rang and Burt picked it up.

"MAIT team, Captain Burton speaking. May I help you?"

There was a long pause as Burt listened intently to the person on the other end.

"Yes sir."

There was another pause as he sat at attention and listened.

"Yes sir." He said and hung up the phone.

"That was Sixth Army. We're supposed to fly to the Presidio on Monday for a conference of some kind." He said.

"DJ, try to find a cheap motel somewhere close to the Presidio and make some reservations. We'll be there a week. I'll get the plane tickets." He said.

It was a seven o'clock flight Monday morning to San Francisco. I don't think we need to get up at that time just to fly across the country, but what do I know?

The flight connected in Denver and Los Angeles, where we spent forty five minutes in each terminal running for the next plane. Lots of fun. We arrived in the San Francisco airport at ten thirty in the morning. There was a fog hanging like a big gray overcoat all around the city on the water.

We caught a cab into town to the Bel-Air motel, which is only a block off Van Ness Street and just about ten or twelve blocks from the Presidio main gate. When we got to the motel, Burt immediately called for a ride to the base.

We were shown into the conference room by a Sergeant and our names were on placards at the main table. Mine said "DJ McAllister Wichita. The Sergeant made the introductions of the people at the table.

"And this is Mike DiStephano, our resident authority on San Francisco." He said.

You would not believe how Mike was dressed. Velvet, no kidding, a velvet suit in dark green with green patent leather shoes, green socks, white shirt, and green tie. All the clothes matched and looked very expensive. He looked like he was some kind of model for a men's clothing store.

It looked like we were just in time because the room filled up right away and a full bull called the conference to order.

"General Williams has been advised of the progress of the MAIT teams over the whole of the Sixth Army area, which as you know, there have been nothing but failing reports written. He has made the decision to implement a recurring inspection policy as had been used in previous years." He said.

"This policy has been endorsed by Major General Atkins, Readiness Region VIII Commander, and Major General Longfellow, Readiness Region IX Commander. The Generals have concluded that there should be evaluation teams similar to the old CMMI teams to evaluate the readiness and provide appropriate reports to the various commanders, especially to the Arcom Commanders."

"Region IX has ordered the team located in San Francisco to be converted to Team number one, and Region VIII has picked the team located at the 89th Arcom to be his Team number two." He said.

"You people sitting here are now hereby transferred to Headquarters Sixth Army and will report to the DCSLOG Colonel Currie. And now let me present Colonel Currie." He said and found a seat.

With that he found his chair and I got a sinking feeling in my stomach. I looked at Rod and Gary and they looked a little sick too.

A man sitting in the rear of the room stood up and walked to the head of the table and gave us his "Welcome to Sixth Army" speech. He talked for nearly an hour explaining in great detail what the mission was and why we were called on to do this and what our new duties would be.

In a nutshell we were going to inspect all the Army Reserve units located in the fifteen western states and report our findings to every level of command up to and including Sixth Army Headquarters. They picked these two teams only because they happened to be located at the flagpoles.

Team one will have seven states and we will have the other eight. There are a hundred and forty units in the eighty ninth and no telling how many in the ninety sixth. The 96th Arcom Headquarters is located in Salt Lake and I've always wanted to go there, so I'm looking forward to that part of the job.

Colonel Currie was still standing and looked like he was trying to think of something. Then he got it.

"You men from Wichita, I would like for you to change your itinerary and stop in Salt Lake to inspect the artillery units there. See Captain Chapman for your TR and tickets. He has your schedule. Thanks a lot. See you soon".

With that he took his seat and now we have eight big artillery units located on Fort Douglas to do on the way home.

The next day, someone was supposed to pick us up at the IHOP and take us to the Post.

Six am comes early when you fly all day and drink all night. Shower, shave, get dressed. I think I'll go down to the office and get a paper and a map of the city. The guy at the desk found me a map under the counter and I walked back to my room.

I had just opened the door to my room when I heard a female voice from behind me say.

"What do you think you're doing?"

I turned around to see the maid talking to a girl coming out of room 105.

"I was just leaving, thank you very much!" She said in a nasty tone.

"You just go on and get out of here!" The maid said.

In the morning, I leave my door open so I can hear when the other guys are going for breakfast. Here they come, I can hear the footsteps. The door to 105 opened and out stepped Burt. So that's why he was gone early. With a beautiful wife like he has, and he's out picking up stuff off the street? He's not as smart as he thinks he is. Hell! He's not as smart as I am. He just got lowered six grades of smart.

We had breakfast at the IHOP around the corner with Rod and Gary complaining of a terrible headache. The pretty green van was there to pick us up right at seven fifteen.

When we arrived at the conference, I made it a point to sit next to Mike. I couldn't miss him, he was red today. Anyone that dresses like this must have a plan, and I need to know what it is. I need all the help I can get.

I leaned over and whispered to him. "What's with the clothes?"

"No one ever questions my judgment. Whatever I say, they believe. I'm always right. Can't beat that, can you?" He said with a big smile.

He went on to prove it to me as soon as the meeting began. I couldn't wear the kind of clothes that he does, but I could get a three piece suit and try out his theory. Maybe an outrageous color or design. I'll look around.

For the next three days we sat through meetings listening to Colonels and Majors talk about their problems with the reserves and what they thought would fix them.

I made it a point to get close to Mike and ask as many questions as I could. You would be surprised at the answers he gave me. I'll tell you as we go along.

About noon on the third day, Rod was saying to Gary and I that he has noticed that Burt has sure been watching the girls around here. I mentioned about the girl coming out of the room on Tuesday morning, and how good looking his wife was.

"What do you mean, you met his wife?" Gary said.

"Yeah, we did." Rod said.

"When?"

"At the O Club that time." I said.

"What time?"

"Oh come on Gary, the gorgeous babe in the O Club when we first got here." Rod said.

"I didn't see a gorgeous babe."

"Damn! You must be blind!" We both said.

When the conference was over, Mike offered to show us a really good seafood restaurant down by Fisherman's Wharf, so we took him up on his offer.

He'll pick us up at five at the motel. Five o'clock came and as good as his word, Mike was sitting outside in one of those beautiful green vans waiting for us. We all piled in and he took us to a place where the food was so good that we all overate so bad that we hurt.

I had abalone, I'm not sure what it is, I always thought it was a shell, but it sure was good. Mike drove us around for a while after dinner and showed us some of the sights in the Marina district, Ghirardelli Square, the Wharf, the Fine Arts Center. We even drove down Lombard Street. What a kick!

Then he dropped us off at a little bar called Bachelors just down the street from the motel. We all went inside and talked to the owner, Max and his barmaid. After a couple of drinks, I figured it was time for me to get out of here and into the fresh air before I did something stupid again.

"I'll see you later. I'm going out to look around a while." I said.

I went out on Chestnut and down the street, here's another bar. Funny place San Francisco, they leave the doors open all the time. I realize that it is summer now, but we have been here in December and all the same doors were open then too.

Here's a bookstore, a Chinese restaurant, I'll stop and look at the menu, another bar, a skin flick, another bar, a grocery store, think I'll get an apple, another restaurant, good apple, but now I need someplace to put the core. There doesn't seem to be any trash cans on the street. There was a cat scavenging in the gutter, I threw the core toward it.

I turned left on Scott and up to the corner. Scott's Seafood is on the corner, the menu really looks good, across the street there's a sign in the window of an Italian place that says "Linguine in Clam sauce, $6.95". I always wanted to try that, guess I know where I'll eat tomorrow.

By the time I got back to the bar, Burt was gone and Rod and Gary were well on their way to a nice buzz. After I had another drink or two, it was going on ten so I decided to call it a night. But Rod and Gary said they were going to stay.

On Thursday, we were taken to a reserve center up north of Sausalito somewhere. We were told they would be teaching us how to inspect the various types of special USAR equipment. We've been inspecting the various types of USAR equipment now for several months, but now they're going to show us how to do it?

I should have known. Nobody is here to show us how to do anything. It's just, 'do an inspection on this unit and write the report'. Whoever was supposed to meet us was too busy to bother with us. Same old Army stuff.

We spent the whole week with Rod and Gary complaining about their headache at breakfast every day. They are going to the base in the morning, lunch at a local café and back to the conference room in the afternoon and the dinner at one of the nice restaurants in the Marina district, and drinking too much in one of the local bars until they stagger back to the room.

I have no sympathy for either of them.

When the call came in from Sixth Army last week to come to the conference, we were told to plan to fly back Saturday. So I made reservations to leave SFO for ten am Saturday morning. That would put us back in Wichita about four pm that day, but now that's all changed.

The conference broke up at lunch on Friday with Captain Chapman handing Burt the tickets to Salt Lake and Wichita.

"Looks like we have a free night in the big city. Where do you want to go?" Burt said.

Mike, our driver and all-knowing guide for the week, leaned over with that look in his eye. You know the one.

"Why don't you go down to North Beach?" He said.

We all looked at each with that same dumb look we have had in the past. I shrugged my shoulders.

"Sure, let's go."

"OK, North Beach here we come." Mike said.

North Beach in San Francisco is an area of skin flicks, bars, with and without live shows, adult book stores and anything else that might trip your trigger. Chinatown is only a couple of blocks away from this unconventional part of town. Mike dropped us off and told us where to get a bus back to the motel and left.

He had made plans to meet with a new girlfriend in an hour and refused to be late. The four of us drifted down one street and up another, looking in the bars and bookstores, listening to the barkers trying to get us into the shows, and finally we went over to China-town and stopped in a little Chinese restaurant.

We had a fantastic dinner in that little Chinese place. I had Moo Goo Gai Pan. The rest of them had I-don't-know-what-and-don't-care for dinner. They said it was good and they got filled up. Sounds good.

After dinner we decided to take another turn around the area, Burt and I are walking together when two girls walked by us.

"Hi boys. How's every little thing?"

We both stopped in our tracks because we're not used to this kind of talk from girls. Rod and Gary had been behind us about ten paces and just as we turned around, the girls spoke to them as they walked by.

We waited for them to catch up. Rod was the first to speak.

"How did he look to you?" Rod asked.

"What?" We said in unison.

"Those two guys." He said and pointed to the two girls walking down the street.

"Didn't you know that?" He laughed.

It's time for me to go home!

Chapter 7

Salt Lake City

It was a short flight to Salt Lake City, and once we retrieved our bags and ran to catch a cab to the GSA motor pool, it looked like things might slow down. It was only a short walk to the car rental place.

"Wait a minute. I think we'll be needing two cars, put one in my name and one in his." The Captain said at the last minute and pointed to Rod. Then we ran to check in to the motel. Then we ran for dinner. I'm beginning to hate all this running.

Fort Douglas clings to the side of a hill up Fourth South Street in Salt Lake. The Fort was founded October 16, 1861 by President Abraham Lincoln and was named for Steven Douglas. Douglas was well known for his debates with Abraham Lincoln on the subject of slavery.

The buildings around Soldiers Circle up the hill are numbered starting from 102 to 108. They are all two story brick barracks built in 1905. Building 100 was built years later in 1932 by the Civilian Conservation Corps.

There are mostly artillery units and the various necessary artillery support units located there, as well as AMSA One off in a separate area. The University of Utah is on land adjacent to the Fort.

The first day we were there, someone in the first unit we were inspecting said that there were a couple of openings coming up here soon at Fort Douglas.

"Hey guys, there's a couple of jobs that were just advertised yesterday and will be open soon. A nine and an eleven, why don't you see CPO and get the real scoop." He said.

Since I'm the secretary for this group, I found the on-base phone directory and called the Civilian Personnel Office for some information on the rumored openings. The girl on the phone said I should come in to the office and pick up an application.

I walked the distance of four buildings down the hill and found the door labeled CPO. I entered and waited at the counter until someone noticed me.

"May I help you?" Said the girl at the desk closest to the counter.

Her desk was piled high with books and papers in trays. She was dressed in a tan blouse and pants that weren't particularly flattering, but I could tell there was something wonderful lurking there.

"Yes. I'm DJ, I just talked to someone?"

"Yes. That was me." She said with an ornery smile beginning.

She had long brown curly hair, green eyes and a big smile. She stood and walked to the counter in front of me. I can't ever remember having to look up at a girl in my life. Her eyes were just slightly above mine and I stood there swimming in their clear depth with the smell of spring in the room.

"I'm Audrey."

When she spoke, it brought me back to reality.

"I – uh – talked to you earlier."

"You already said that." She said.

She giggled and leaned over toward me.

"How can I help you?" She asked with her voice lowered to almost a whisper.

She must have noticed me swimming. I leaned over and whispered to her. A second whiff of that spring day invaded my being and prompted flashes of fantasies of all kinds.

"Tell me about the vacancies and tell me about yourself." I said quietly.

She smiled coyly and lowered her voice a little more so that only I could hear what she was about to say.

"I'm five foot nine, and with heels six feet. I'm single and I work till four thirty."

"Would you have dinner with me tonight?" I asked.

"No - - -."

There was a long pause before she ended the sentence.

"But I will tomorrow." She said.

Her smile lit up her face. A little wrinkle in that smile told me that she was having a good time at my expense and enjoying it a lot as well.

"Shall I pick you up here at four thirty then?" I asked.

"Good idea, why don't you?" She said.

Her smile turned in to a chuckle now. I turned to go and she reached out and touched my arm.

"Don't you want the forms for those vacancies?"

She laughed out loud and handed me the papers.

When I returned to the unit where we were working, we all examined the paperwork on the jobs. I know I will be applying for one of them, maybe both.

On the way back to the motel, I asked Rod to stop at a hobby shop I saw as we passed it on First South Street.

"May I help you?" The man behind the counter asked.

"Yes. I'm looking for some inexpensive HO brass engines. You have anything?"

"Over here! What brings you to our fair city?" He said.

I walked to the counter he motioned to.

"I'm working at the Fort for a couple weeks on TDY. Could I see those?" I asked and pointed to the ones I meant.

"Oh, yeah? I'm in one of the units there. What're you doing?" He asked.

"Inspection team. You remember the CMMI? That's us now."

He brought two used items out of the case and placed them on the glass countertop. Rod and I examined them very carefully.

"They run?" I asked.

"Of course." He said.

"Original boxes?" I asked.

"Only this one." He said and pointed to it. "Yeah, you're the bad guys. Everyone's heard about you." He said. "Tell you what, if you like them both, forty bucks apiece."

My face must have registered when he said we were the bad guys.

"That's OK, I won't hold it against you. My name's Paul and I'm the manager of this world famous establishment."

I looked more closely at the little engines. The price he just quoted to me was a steal.

"World famous?"

"Well not really. Hey, how'd you like to see the Zephyr come in tonight? I like to get a bite at the Rio Grande Café after I close and then ride the train around the wye when they turn it for the return run. You wanna come?" He asked.

"You bet. And I'll take them both. Will you take a check?"

"Here's a pen." He said.

We finished the deal and Rod and I left with my package.

Paul picked me up at the motel at eight and we went directly to the Rio Grande Station. We had dinner and talked about trains, his wife and kids, and the city until the train rolled in at nine thirty. We walked outside and waited while all the passengers got off the train.

"Come on." He said and jumped onto the step of the observation car. With great reservation, I followed.

"Can you do this?" I asked.

"Sure! I ride up to the wye and back all the time. You ever been on this train?" He asked.

"No."

"Come on."

He ran up the stairs to the domed part of the car. Wow! What a view! We stood there and watched the city as the train made its maneuver through the wye and back to the station. It will sit there all night with the diesels chugging lowly until it departs for the return trip to Denver in the morning. What a kick that was!

On the way to the Fort in the morning I begged for the car from Rod.

"Hot date, DJ?" He said.

"I hope!"

At four thirty sharp, I was waiting outside the door marked 'CPO' until she appeared. I could feel my pulse race as she walked up to me. She was dressed in a bright pink low cut blouse and short skirt. Much better than yesterday. I was right about the something wonderful. I know it is a warm night, but she made my temperature go up without any trouble.

"I'm ready." She said.

This is my first time ever in this city and I don't have a clue about where to go, fortunately she had a special place in mind. It was decorated in 1950's cars and memorabilia and served unusual vegetarian sandwiches. I ate something and listened to her sweet voice. We sat on couches made from 1950's car parts

"Is there anything good playing at the local movie?" I asked.

"Yes, I'll show you." She said.

Once we were seated, I pulled her to me and we were snuggled together for the duration of the film. On the drive to her house, she continued to snuggle against me. I enjoyed it a lot.

"Here it is." She said.

I pulled over and parked in her driveway. I leaned over to kiss her and that kiss lasted twenty minutes before she opened the car door and disappeared into the house.

I saw her every day till we left. On Thursday she said she had tickets to see The Mormon Tabernacle Choir. Thursday is their rehearsal day. I had only heard of them, I never thought I would get to see and hear them live. We were in the nose bleed seats but I could hear every note and the view was spectacular.

After that she picked me up every evening at my room. When she was ready, we had dinner out or at her house and some fun after that.

One night, I remember that we went to a place called Marie Callender's. We had sandwiches. Big sandwiches and a big beautiful piece of banana cream pie. I want to go back there again.

I don't even know what I did in those units for the rest of the week. I got to see a lot of the special sights of the city. I filled out the forms for the GS-11 and left them with Audrey just before we left.

I think we finished all the units on time and only a couple failed. This is one trip I didn't really want to see end. I think my new best friend could grow on me, but she's a thousand miles away.

As much as I dislike Wichita, I am glad to be on the plane going back, a week of fun in San Francisco was enough for me. Colonel Currie said we would be coming to these conferences in June and December from now on. We will have to make our schedules to fit the Colonel's wishes.

I hope he doesn't add trips out of the blue like he did this time. But I really enjoyed this one. Just imagine! A trip like this twice a year, every year, from now on. It's a good thing we'll get some time to recuperate.

The rest of the month was spent in the office making maps and charts of the units we will be tasked with in the eight states which the Colonel so graciously gave us. Each of us was assigned a job we would be doing in the office by the Captain.

I was assigned 'Travel'. That's everything and anything that has to do with the team traveling. Hotel and motel reservations, rental cars, GSA cars, plane tickets and connections, and other duties as assigned. Rod got Finance, Gary got Publication, and Burt will do the scheduling.

The Captain felt that we should all be members of the Reserves there at the Arcom and he did a lot of politicking to find us spots to fill. Rod is retired so he couldn't go in, but Gary and I got roped into saying 'I do' again. I guess that 'we all' meant just the two of us.

Now that we have all the details worked out between us on the team and we have a rapport started with the Arcom Staff, it looks like it's time to go out and rape and pillage the countryside.

Rod and the Captain made out a schedule for the next three months with the help of the Arcom and I have the first months reservations made.

We start in Mitchell, South Dakota, then on to Tucson, Arizona in October and Bismarck, North Dakota in November and I really don't think North

Dakota is the place to be in November, but I don't make those decisions.

Chapter 8

Hutchinson

We, that is, the Captain, decided to stay close to home this week, since we had been out of town for nearly a month. There is a Military Police unit in Hutchinson. Hutchinson, Kansas is about sixty miles northwest up along the Arkansas River from Wichita.

Have I mentioned? I'm a member of a team of inspectors, called War Readiness Assistance Team or WRAT for short. We've been called a bunch of rats more than once. But I'm not the biggest rat. I'm just a little mouse.

We travel the fifteen western states and inspect the Army Reserve for readiness. We have an office in the Arcom Headquarters in Wichita. Our team travels to all the major cities and a lot of the minor ones in eight states. We have the Dakotas, Nebraska, Kansas, New Mexico, Colorado, Utah and Wyoming. We are supposed to look at each unit every year, but that is impossible.

Our schedule is really strange. We are usually out of town for ten to fourteen days, and in town for a week. We normally work out the final details on the Monday before we leave. Then we leave on Tuesday. We are scheduled to work that week, the weekend, and the following week and then arrive back home on Friday.

That makes eleven days on the road. That's not so bad, unless we have problems with the weather or in the case of Fredonia, unforeseen circumstances.

On Monday the Captain called the unit to notify them that we would be inspecting them on Tuesday. We spent the rest of the day getting everything ready for the trip.

It's about an hour's drive under normal conditions. But, there seems to be nothing normal in our lives anymore. If we drive up along the river, there are a dozen little towns and narrow roads to navigate through. None of us mentioned this fact and Rod is driving this time.

Rod started out driving and we were doing very well. If we go the long way, up the interstate to Newton and across on US 50, which are much better roads, the time will be the same, but the mileage will be more. And none of us will say anything about the roads or distance.

We left Tuesday at seven thirty to make the short drive in our pretty green car. It was pleasant for a cold month, and we arrived about an hour later.

Rod put the car on seventy miles per hour once we found the Interstate, it didn't take long to make it to Newton. Then another thirty miles along Highway fifty and we were walking into the Hutchinson Army Reserve Center. I know because it said so on a big sign out front.

I am sure the Captain will be timing us on this one. It's our first inspection since the conference that he will actually be involved in. He didn't do much in

Salt Lake except stand around and look like he knew what was going on, but he didn't.

The unit doesn't have much as far as equipment is concerned. A few weapons, a jeep, and a few miscellaneous items. Rod did find something. One of the badges was missing. When the Captain told the Sergeant in Charge about it, they looked all through the desks and arms room and they magically found it somewhere they had just looked. When the captain picked it up, he noticed the badge was warm to his touch. It just shows you that magic is real.

It took us all morning to finish the unit. The guys in the unit were ready to go to lunch. So we obliged them and hurried out to find something for ourselves.

After a short lunch, we sat down and finished writing the report by one thirty and the Captain really put on his first performance for us. The outbrief took about thirty minutes, and we were walking out to the car.

The Captain insisted that he drive back, and that he would take the shorter route. None of us knew how he had found a Kansas map and that he was studying it to see where we were in the state.

We left Hutch at three o'clock and after an amusing, sometimes downright funny tour on K-96 along the river, we arrived two hours later. But in all fairness, we got to see Elmer, Yoder, passed by Haven and Mount Hope. We hit the outskirts of town near Maize and on into Wichita's west side. Rod was especially amused since he is the only one of us who is a Kansas resident.

All three of us knew better that to let the Captain hear us laughing at him and his cursing and swearing at the roads and the little towns and open land. We tried to tell him, but he is a Captain, and Commander. And he knows better. And he will tell you so. Over and over.

He delivered the report to DCSLOG when we arrived at the office. The building was empty by then so he just left it on the desk.

We'll be working half days for the rest of the week. He said it took everything out of him on this trip. Wait till he sees what's coming.

I always wanted to build a special car of my own. I couldn't do it before, because the Captain always wanted to be the ruler of us and our time. He felt that we should eat, sleep and drink whatever the Government says twenty-four seven.

Now that I have my own house and no more prying eyes looking over my shoulder at every little thing I do, I can begin my project.

This car should get good gas mileage, be easy to work on when trouble shows up and comfortable to drive. I don't think that's too much to ask. I decided on a Volkswagen based running gear. Maybe a kit car.

I would like to have something that wasn't a copy of everything else I have ever seen. It needs to be special looking too. It took me a long time to find just the right one, but I finally did. A VW based 1940 Ford Woodie Wagon.

I have no idea how I will get this car built, but I'll try. And I'm committed. Maybe I should be committed.

Chapter 9

AMSA

While we're figuring out how to do stuff, we are doing inspections too. What a laugh. The inspection this week is on the AMSA in the back yard. If we walk slow, it will take us six minutes to get there, leaving seven hours and fifty four minutes to work for the rest of the day.

Dusty has a coffee pot always going, but he doesn't have donuts or rolls, so I bought a dozen donuts at Dunkin' on the way in and took them to him in his office before the team attacked the AMSA.

When we finally did go there, Dusty made a production of offering a donut to each of us and the Captain never was the wiser.

The Captain introduced each of us to the guys in the shop and told what our areas of expertise were. Gene, Dusty and I were smiling, but we didn't offer anything. He continued as if it were a meeting and explained in detail, what we do and who we work for. I suppose that was supposed to impress them.

I explained in the office yesterday that we want to go really slow and enlist as much help from them as we possibly can. We will need it in the future. If you find a discrepancy, show it to them and explain why it is bad and don't write it up unless it can't be fixed while we are there.

We looked at every piece of equipment and every piece of paper. I was with Gene all day and we did the Facility and Safety potion of the inspection. If I found anything that looked suspicious, I told him about it and showed him how to fix it, or where to find it right then. Rod and Gary did all the equipment with the other guys. Dusty and the Captain were in the office with all the paperwork.

We decided at the beginning that we would stop at noon and come back the next day, until we were done. So at noon Tuesday, we packed it up and walked slowly back to our office and went home.

Wednesday was a bright new day and we started again. We finished up by ten but we all stood around and shot the bull till eleven thirty till we could go home again.

Thursday was the day we actually wrote the report and outbriefed it. When the Captain was done, he carried the report down the hall to the Colonel. We gave the AMSA the highest rating that we have available. The Colonel was very pleased about that.

I searched for months in every VW catalog and magazine I could find to find a fiberglass hood and fenders that looked like the 40 Ford but were made for the VW. Gene had a catalog where I finally found them.

A company in California had the exact parts that I wanted. I ordered all the parts as soon as I could.

I found a custom fit fiberglass dash and console for a VW in the same catalog and ordered it the same day. This dash will mean that I have to move all the gauges and controls, but I think it will be worth it.

Now I'm waiting for the hood, fenders and dash to be delivered. I got real lucky, the grill will come with the hood.

One thing in the early inspection of the older VW's was this. The metal floors acquire rust quickly. I don't want to buy more parts for the floors if I don't have to. Gene will know the answer.

Chapter 10

USAR School

The powers that be have decreed that every USAR unit in the nation will be inspected, that is evaluated, once every year. We, as lowly peons, must then comply.

That's enough of my smart aleck talk. We will give a look at all of them. Some, like the one today, will not need, or even be able to be inspected properly.

Down the hall four doors away is a USAR School. They are tasked with teaching the Arcom's units classes handed down by the Commanders of the Army, Regions, or ARCOMS.

They actually do not own enough equipment to call it equipment. There are desks and chairs, writing utensils and notebooks or paper of some kind and various publications. Of course they must have a Publications Account.

There are a number of 'teachers' in the unit. No weapons, no vehicles, no tools, unless you count the pencil sharpener.

They have their own uniforms, but no maintenance is required.

But here we are, walking into the school office. Funny, it looks a lot like our office. I told the Officer in Charge last week that we would be doing this and he smiled as much as I did about it.

I don't know how we can stretch this out to look like we are doing something, but we will try.

We carefully examined every little item in their office. Pictures on the wall, chips in the paint, the paint color, the floor tile and its color. Everything possible. Everything passed.

The School passed in every area with the highest score. We won't have to sit around here in this office for another year. I think the instructors at the School all think we are crazy, but we explained it in great detail to them, and they finally got it.

The School has one of those special green cars with the writing on the doors that they received from the Arcom, but of course, that little item is not inspectable either.

With us working half days at home, I can get a lot done on my new car project. Now I have to find a VW for the donor car. There are a lot of them in this town, so it shouldn't be a big problem.

Gene offered to help me find the right car for my project. He knows where most of them are, he said. Almost every day he came in to our office with an ad for a VW for sale.

It can't be a Super Beetle, it has to be one of the first generation. I want one with Independent Rear Suspension (IRS). The IRS gives a smoother ride and better cornering.

I finally found one with all the niceties I wanted and the right price. But it is orange! With a horrible green interior! Why would someone do that?

Gene went with me to pick it up and to drive it to my garage for me. As soon as he saw it he began to laugh.

"How much did you pay for this? Are you sure you want to do this? Does it really run or do I have to push it to your place?" He said.

He was laughing the whole time and even when we pulled into my driveway. Too bad it wasn't raining, that would have calmed him down.

But now the real work begins. He said he would help me anytime I needed it. I really appreciate that. I haven't learned how to weld yet.

Chapter 11

Tuscon

We went to Fort Huachuca a day early because the weather services all around the country were talking about El Nino and the big rains that might be on tap.

You don't even think about rain when you visit Arizona. The name even means 'dry place'. So when the weatherman talks about a big rain around someplace south of Phoenix, you smile a lot and laugh it off. But this time they were right.

Once we entered the motor pool all four of us noticed among the M-60 tanks there were two that stood out like beacons. An M-88 Armored Recovery Vehicle, and an AVLB, Armored Vehicle Launch Bridge. These two must be magnetic, because we were all drawn to them across the motor pool. I had to touch them.

The bridge has a sixty foot long steel bridge folded in half and mounted on top of an M-60 chassis so that the bridge can be unfolded across a creek, river or canyon that will support the weight of the M-60 tanks crossing it. Then it will cross it and pick it up on the other side, retract the bridge to the top and move on with the other tanks.

The M-88 is equally hulking and heavy, but is used as a tank tow truck when one of them stops running. Where the tank only has seven hundred and fifty horsepower, the tow truck has over a thousand and will easily tow another tank.

The M-60 tank weighs about sixty tons and is twenty three feet long by twelve feet wide and eleven feet high. It is quite a huge piece of machinery. With the bridge mounted on top of it, the weight goes up sharply.

We flew to Tucson then drove to Sierra Vista to our motel and I collapsed on the bed. It was a long trip with the flying into Tucson and driving ninety miles to the Fort and getting a good look at the motor pool.

It rained all night and was still raining in the morning when we went for breakfast. Good thing I brought a good coat and hat.

It is expected that when we visit a unit that is on our list to be inspected, we make a stop with the command structure and do an inbriefing for them so they know what to expect from us.

Once the niceties were finished, all of us, including the Commander walked out to the motor pool. I don't know if the others noticed it, but I did. The bridge is missing! There is a big vacancy between two of the tanks. You would have to be blind not to notice it. I wanted to see it extend and retract the bridge itself.

The Commander and his staff noticed it right away and two of them walked to where several troops were standing and began to ask them where it was. I saw a lot of head shaking and shoulder shrugging and I knew they were lying.

You can't move something that huge that makes that much noise without someone noticing it.

Rod had a brilliant idea.

"Come on, DJ. Let's take a ride."

We stepped into the nearest Jeep and we were off. We took our time winding through the back roads and trails until we found it. They are narrow dirt trails cut through the forested area between the Fort and the Mexican border. Most of them are far too narrow for a huge machine like an M-60.

But there it was! A sixty ton hulking piece of metal nightmare in a ditch on its side. Someone obviously knew that there was something wrong with it and that it would not pass the inspection, so they tried to hide it. The only trouble with the hiding place was that it was easy to see, from any angle.

The back woods trails were muddy and hard to manage. No doubt the bridge began to skid around a bend and toward the side of the road and the driver couldn't correct it. I think someone must have got hurt in this mishap. There is a crew of four to run this beauty. Where are they?

Now Rod is an easy going kind of a guy, but when he saw this monster, he began to laugh. Not a grin, or a chuckle, but a full blown belly laugh. We stood there in the woods laughing at it until someone must have heard us and came in another jeep.

"You got a clipboard and a pad, DJ?" He said.

I pulled one out of the jeep and began to write.

"Road wheels not touching the ground. That's an X! Multiple fluid leaks. Another X." He pointed to the engine compartment where fluids of all kinds were pouring out. "Unable to perform its mission. Another X." By this time he was all smiles. He ultimately wrote ten X's on the bridge.

An X is a bad thing in an inspection. It means Failure with a capital X. This one has ten of them.

The Commander and his staff found us in the middle of all the fun we were having and blew his stack.

"What are you doing?" He yelled. This guy was beginning to sound like our Captain. I began to smile at that thought. Then soon Rod and I were both laughing again.

"What the hell are you laughing about?" He is sounding more like the Captain every minute.

We told him what was so funny and he chuckled a little. I told him that they were his men trying to protect themselves from a failing grade and he began to laugh a little. Then I pointed to the 'pickup truck' in the ditch and he saw the humor.

"I'll tell you what Colonel! If your Battalion can get this thing out of the ditch, into the motor pool, cleaned up and running, you will pass this inspection." Rod said. "If not, then you have a problem."

Rod and I took the jeep back to the motor pool and went on to other things we could do.

I really wanted to pull that old joke on someone, but Rod didn't have the heart to do it. It goes like this.

"Hey guy would you check the air in that tire on that road wheel. It might need air." The tires on the six road wheels on each side are solid rubber and no air is needed.

Rod and I drove a few of the various vehicles and inspected a few. I really wanted to drive one of the APC's. That is an M-113 Armored Personnel Carrier. It's a big aluminum can with a big door in the back that falls down and the troops run in or out as they want. It's hot in the summer and cold in the winter, but it's all the Army has for the job.

Sierra Vista has a few good places to eat and Rod and I tried them all, one by one. Each day breakfast, lunch and dinner, then on to another one.

We did all the weapons, and the electronics that we could find. We decided not to look for anything that might not be in its regular place. After what's happened so far, that would get too complicated.

We spent all day during the rain writing up all of our notes. The Colonel made it a point to find Rod and I and show us the bridge in the motor pool. The rain had helped to clean it, but we could see that they spent a lot of time getting it ready for us. It looked really good. He had the crew start it for us and extend it out onto the ground and retract it.

The Colonel was very relieved when we told him that his motor pool had passed, and that we would write it up that way.

It took us an extra day to wait for the weather to clear enough for us to get out of Sierra Vista and on up to Tucson and catch a plane going our way.

After the plane set down in Wichita, I breathed a sigh of relief. It was a long trip, and difficult, but there was some fun sprinkled in, too. I piled into my car and ran home to bed.

I didn't get much done this time on the car project. We didn't have enough time between trips to do much. I'm still working on finding all the things that I might need somewhere farther along in this project.

Chapter 12

Mitchell

Gary is still in the reserves, but he had to transfer to a unit in Wichita in order to stay in and satisfy the wishes of our esteemed commander, the Captain. His unit was located in Mitchell, South Dakota. We are on our way there this week. To hear Gary talk, Mitchell is the best place anywhere. He called a few friends to tell them that we were on our way, and to be ready for an inspection.

He conveniently forgot to tell the Captain about that call, and Rod and I have remained silent. Mitchell is a long drive, about four hundred and seventy miles. Without even looking, I know that we could go up I-35 to Topeka, then on to St. Joseph and I-29 all the way to Sioux Falls, then I-90 to Mitchell.

But the Captain will want to drive up US-81 all the way. Back roads and little towns, what fun. What should have taken eight hours, took more than ten. But I had made reservations at the Mitchell Holiday Inn prior to our arrival. Am I glad I did. The room is great and I fell on the bed and had a little nap right away. If the unit is as good as this bed, we're going to have a good day tomorrow.

Everyone in the unit was on top of their game and I didn't find even the smallest problem. And I really tried. Rod and Gary couldn't even find dirt on the floors of the vehicles. One of the guys told me that he vacuumed all the vehicles to make sure they were clean.

Someone must have scared all these units. I wouldn't have thought that they would be this good.

Gary introduced Rod and I to all his friends in the unit and later in town when we came across one. Gary asked about a guy named Daniel Thomas. No one seemed to be able to say that they had seen him in several days since the last drill.

We moved on with the inspection and listened to the Captain give orders, more silly stuff. You can tell that he likes to be in charge. It took another day to finish everything and begin to write the report. A few of the guys took us to see the Corn Palace in the downtown area. Very impressive.

When we were done and as we were leaving to get packed for the run to the Capital city of Pierre (pronounced PIER), they told us about the fantastic steaks at a certain restaurant in town. The Captain perked up and said that would be where we would go tonight for dinner.

I have been given the task of driving in the various towns. Why? I don't know, but I can drive if no one else wants to do it. My trade-off is that I do not drive on the open road. We arrived at the restaurant and when I parked, I noticed the lot was full of those long low concrete parking bumpers used to stop the car from over-riding into the car in the lane in front of you. I pulled into a space and shut off the car, and we bailed out.

The guys were right, the food was fabulous, the price was right and we were very satisfied when we left. But now comes the problem you won't believe. We all piled in the car with Rod and Gary in their customary positions in the back. The Captain always sits in front ready to direct our every move.

The rain decided to fall while we were inside. So to add to our distress, it is wet and coming down pretty good.

I started the car and put it in reverse, and began to back out of the space.

"What are you doing?" Screamed the Captain.

I stepped on the brake.

I don't call him Burt anymore, he's too much of a jerk for me to get too close to him.

"I'm pulling out of the parking lot." I said.

"Go forward!" He yelled again and pointed with his arm lunged forward.

"But, there's a"

He stopped me in mid sentence.

"I don't want to hear excuses! Go forward!" He yelled again.

"But, there's"

He stopped me again.

"No buts! That's an order! A direct order!" He yelled and waved his arms.

"OK. Here we go." I said.

Rod and Gary had seen the parking bumpers in the lot when we arrived and now they both had seat belts on and were holding fast to anything that was available.

I put it in 'forward' and hit the gas. I probably hit the gas too hard, but if you're going to have fun, you might as well do it right. That green Chevy spun the wheels on the wet pavement and lunged forward over the first block like a Monster Truck at a rally.

"BANG! CRASH! THUD!"

Then the rear wheels came over.

"BUMP! CRUNCH! THUMP!"

Then we hit the bumper for the other row with the front wheels.

"BANG! CRASH! THUD!"

Then the rear wheels again.

"BANG! CRASH! THUD! SLAM!"

The car finally made it out of the forest and onto dry land. That is, the wet level pavement. Rod and Gary were in stitches. They had been yelling and bouncing and falling one way then the other and feigning injuries. They yelled that they were hurt and they were going to sue me for emotional distress. I could tell the Captain was yelling something because I could see that his mouth was open, but I couldn't hear a thing.

When we finally stopped, the Captain was screaming at the top of his lungs to stop.

" "WHAT THE HELL WAS THAT? WHY DIDN'T YOU STOP WHEN I TOLD YOU TO?" He was yelling again.

"I was only following your orders, Sir." I said calmly.

"Why didn't you tell me there were those things in the way?" He's still yelling. Rod and Gary are still laughing and bouncing around.

"I tried twice, but you wouldn't listen, Sir." I said.

"I should write you up for that!" He said.

"I wish you would." I said and I smiled.

He shut up then, but he was pissed all the way to Pierre. Too bad.

I think it was finally starting to sink into his head, but there's no way to tell for sure. Good times in Mitchell.

Pierre is the Capital City and is about two hundred and twenty five miles west on Interstate Ninety. It was a pleasant drive with no screaming and yelling, I was still smiling. We found the motel and parked. Rod, Gary and I had been silent for the whole drive. No sense starting another yelling match.

When Rod parked, I noticed several GSA cars and cars with badges and lettering saying they were police cars. I looked closely inside at one and saw three letters on a piece of paper, FBI. That'll give you a shiver even if you are a good guy.

When we walked in to the motel office, there were several guys sitting around in the chairs and the clerk behind the counter. The Captain told the clerk who we were and that we had reservations. All the men in the chairs stood up and moved behind us.

"You are Captain Burton? One of them asked.

"Yes, I am." The Captain said.

"Come with me." He said, he had his gun in hand and put handcuffs on him.

"Which one is Andersson?" One of the FBI agents said. He had a forty five at the ready.

Rod and I pointed to Gary and I got a little chill down my back. This is not looking good for us.

He handcuffed Gary and they took him into the back office. They took the Captain into another office farther back in the motel.

The Marshall who was left with us said we should sit, so we sat and kept silent. I was glad he didn't pull out a gun for us too. I have no idea what is going on, but I'm not about to ask any questions or say a word.

It was five or ten minutes before we heard any noise at all, and I heard laughing. What is this? There's no laughing when you're being handcuffed. That's a rule. The motel office door opened and out walked Gary, his FBI agent and another man we hadn't seen yet. And they were all smiling. And no handcuffs were to be seen.

"Rod, DJ, this is Daniel Thomas. He is the Chief of the South Dakota State Police, and a very old friend of mine." He looked at Daniel and said. "I think this was very funny after all the pranks I've pulled on you, but you scared these guys out of their wits. I can only imagine what the Captain is thinking." Gary said.

"He is being told how to treat people. I have a list of issues that one of the Marshalls and an FBI agent are straightening out with him. Things will start to get better very soon." Daniel said. "Or else! He wouldn't like me when I'm angry."

Funny. He didn't look like the Hulk, but I'll bet he could if he wanted to.

Russ must have told the chief about the parking bumpers in Mitchell.

Later, we found out that all the FBI and US Marshalls were in town for a murder trial. I don't watch the news very much, so I wasn't up on all the information about it, but the others were. Some of them were witnesses, some of them were the Security for the people in the courtroom and some were just there to help if needed.

The long drive back to Wichita was chilly and quiet. I rather enjoyed it, but I'm sure someone else didn't.

It took a lot of time to find extenders for the wheels that would fit the VW and allow Ford five bolt fifteen inch wheels to be mounted. The fiberglass fenders that I bought were so wide that the little VW wheels and tires looked lost.

Once I installed the spacers, I had to buy the Ford wheels and tires and prepare the wheels for paint. Again I got lucky. The tires were nearly brand new and were exactly the size that I wanted. I bought everything at a salvage yard and had them take the tires off of the rims so I could paint them.

I wanted to get everything fitted and painted before I got started in earnest. "And don't forget to paint the wheels." I told myself.

I can see that it will take a lot of time to sand and prepare these wheels for paint. Oh well. What else do I have to do?

Chapter 13

Denver

We are flying to Denver this week to inspect a MASH unit, and what better place to find one than at Fitzsimmons Army Hospital. Fitz is a huge hospital in the middle of town. It has always taken care of our vets and others associated with the military services.

We will land at Stapleton Airport at ten twenty seven and drive to a nice motel where I have reserved our rooms. Unless, that is, the Captain does something stupid like he has been doing lately.

We picked up a rental car at the airport and because we are in a city, I am driving. To get to the motel, I will go straight down Quebec Street and turn right at Colfax and we'll be there. After we throw our clothes into the rooms, we'll go shake hands and smile a lot.

On the way down Quebec, the Captain spotted Fitzsimmons Hospital just as we were passing it. He has never been here and didn't know anything about the city, county, or state. But that doesn't bother him. He doesn't know anything about most things out here in the west.

"There it is!" He yelled. "Turn here! Quick! Turn Here! That's an order!" He's yelling again. "Dammit, that's an order!" He yelled again. He's yelling and waving his hands.

Now we all know when he yells "That's an order", we should immediately stop whatever we are doing and do as he commands. So, I did!

There's a city bus coming north on Quebec about four car lengths from us. I yanked the wheel to the left and we shot across the median and the two lanes of traffic in front of the bus and into the entrance of the Hospital complex at thirty five miles per hour. It seemed like eighty when I was crossing in front of that bus. I'll bet the bus driver crapped his pants when he saw us.

I'm smiling. They are all aghast with their mouths open and crazy noises coming out.

He's going to start yelling again as soon as his heart starts beating again.

"What the hell are you doing? That bus could have hit us!"

"So what? It was on your side." I said.

That shut him up immediately. And the look on his face was priceless.

I kept driving until we were parked in front of the Admin building. I turned off the car and opened the door to get out. He was still yelling but I turned off my ears to him, since it was all baloney. He stopped to take a breath and I said.

"Captain, I don't have to listen to any more of your crap. I quit! I will call the General and tell him that I quit because I can't work with you anymore!"

I turned around and began to walk to the door when Rod and Gary jumped out of the car and ran to stop me.

"Wait! If you leave, we'll be out of a job and we can't afford that." Rod said. "Let us get rid of this clown and we will work things out. I promise."

"Alright! I will finish this trip, but I don't see anything happening any time soon." I said.

"I guarantee by the time of the next conference, he will be out or on his way." Rod said. "Besides it is only a couple of months till we go to San Fran again."

We stood and talked for a few minutes, and decided that we would go co the units here and work it out between ourselves before we do anything foolish.

"Do you two know which motel we are in here?"

"No." Rod said.

"It's the Best Western down the street on Colfax, only a couple blocks." I pointed in the direction of the motel. "I'll try to get there by myself. There must be someone here from the Springs that I can hook up with for this trip. Here's the keys."

None of us spoke to the Captain for the rest of the day and when they checked in they didn't offer to go to dinner with him. Rod said that he would talk to him later. Rod and Gary continued to try to make peace.

"Well, I'll make it simple for you. It's him or me!" I said.

For the rest of the week, I did my part of the unit and wrote it up. When I was done, I found someone to talk to and had a very good time. I found a couple of people who were from the Springs or had relatives who lived there or knew people who lived there. We had lots of good discussions about our mutual interests.

Ever since I watched MASH on TV, I have enjoyed talking to the doctors and nurses there. The reasons that motivate people to enter the Military Services have always fascinated me. Every one of the doctors and nurses that I have talked to said they did it to help people. I would never want to be in the medical business. Too much blood.

In contrast, every one of the grunts and people like me have said that they did it because they were drafted or their time had come.

We have found out, over the last few months that this team is not a democracy. The Captain is the absolute ruler. He wants to be one of the boys, but he also insists that we obey him unconditionally and immediately. So we do. As far as that goes. He found that out today. But he is going to be in for a rude awakening one of these days. I guarantee that! I wonder how other people get along with him? We shall see.

I told Rod that since I have my own plane ticket, they shouldn't look for me during the flight to Wichita. I might catch a different plane. That would shake up our dear Captain.

I found a little time to work on my car project that always seems to be there waiting for me.

I stripped the car inside and out of everything, carpet, seats, upholstery, headliner, windows, lights, trim, gauges, steering wheel, engine and shrouding, wheels, tires, and put it up on blocks. I took off all four fenders and the front and rear hood as well.

I had to buy a special tool to break rusted nuts off of the bolts. It came in very handy here. There was a lot more rust than I thought. Not so much that I had to replace any of the metal parts, but more than I expected.

Chapter 14

Bismarck

The schedule says that we are supposed to go to Bismarck this month. Nobody goes to Bismarck in November on purpose. It snows there. It really snows there. I would think that's a given.

I don't have any travel plans yet. I can make motel reservations, maybe. I need more information.

"What's the deal on Bismarck, Captain?" I asked.

"Nothing much. We can drive up and stay at that nice hotel in the middle of town. We'll only be a short drive from Fort Lincoln where the unit is located. No sweat." He said.

I'm not liking this very much and it's going to get worse, I'll bet. To drive this trip, it is about eight hundred miles to Bismarck. That's a two day trip. But I only drive in towns, so I'm doing just fine with his decision.

Well we started on Monday since it was such a long drive. Rod started since he was the Kansas guy on the team and we made it all the way to Yankton. Up at six, on the road by seven. We've got over four hundred more miles to cover to get to where we're going.

This is crazy! I could have got a plane ticket and we would have been there by now. From Yankton we drove to Mitchell, Aberdeen, Jamestown, and finally Bismarck. The hotel was easy to find. It's one of the biggest buildings in town. It was after dark when we arrived, but we got checked in and we all hit the sack.

At least the weather was nice. I was up at my usual six o'clock, and cleaned up. I walked leisurely downstairs to see snow on the ground through the hotel's front windows. I asked the clerk how much there was.

"We got a big one last night." He said. "It looks like eight inches and it's still coming down. The TV said there are really big drifts around the area. Maybe not in town, but no one's out yet, so they don't know"

"Great! Just great!" I said to myself.

"Where can I get some breakfast?" I asked the clerk.

"Normally right here, but our cooks and waitresses haven't come to work yet." He said.

"You could walk right up there." He said pointing to a light in the window about a block away. "They are our only competitor in the morning. And I see by the light that they are open."

"Any chance the TV said how long this will last?" I asked.

"Well, normally a snow like this will only last a few days, maybe a week." He said.

"Only a week?" How nice.

I stood around until Rod came down and we started for the little café. Slogging through the snow up to your waist is difficult, but we made it to find the little café was nearly full. Grandma was sitting in the very back peeling potatoes for home fries. We could see the folks in the kitchen were up their ears in orders and trying to get the food out.

Rod and I had two eggs with everything and were nearly finished by the time that Gary and the Captain showed up. We all snow plowed back to the hotel and watched the local news till it said that the plows were clearing off the streets and that it was safe to drive locally.

By ten thirty, the cooks and waitresses had come to work and we could smell food cooking from the kitchen. The desk clerk made it a point to tell us what was on the menu for today. It sounds good.

We arrived at Fort Lincoln just after twelve and found the unit personnel up to their eyeballs with cleanup work. The wind must have been blowing into the motor pool. There were snow drifts over the tops of trucks so that you couldn't recognize what kind of truck it was. One Sergeant said that they had a few deuce and a halfs. We tried to do an inspection on anything that was inside, but it was impossible. Everyone was coming and going constantly and we finally had to give it up.

The Captain finally made a decision that made sense. It's about time. We'll wait until tomorrow to start the inspection. So we laid around the hotel and watched TV for the rest of the day.

Later in the day, the TV news showed the plows out on the streets and roads around Bismarck. Things were beginning to be cleared up.

On the way up, I remember that the Captain said that he wanted to see the little town across the river called Mandan. That trip has not been mentioned since the snow.

It was a good thing that food wasn't far away, we could eat in the hotel now. The next day it was sunny, still cold but better. The unit had cleaned all the snow off of their vehicles, but we still couldn't do much.

We stayed another day until the TV news shows said that the snow was cleaned off of the main roads. Not completely true.

The drive back was ridiculous! We made it to Aberdeen on the first day. There is a nice big red brick building that says 'Holiday Inn' on the sign. After we checked in, we found that it has a heated pool. There were men's bathing suits for sale at the gift shop. Of course, I bought one and soaked myself in the luxurious warmed water for an hour.

The next day we drove straight through. None of us wanted to get caught by the weather again. We'll stay home till the snow is gone.

If I'm going to get this car finished, I must work on something every day that I am in town from another trip.

I sanded every piece of metal I could find. I spent every day on this little job. I sanded, wiped and cleaned until I was sick of it, but I finally got it all cleaned up. It only took ten days, maybe twelve.

Gene came over and welded an extra layer of metal in the floor where the rust attacks it in most of these cars. What a big help that was.

Chapter 15

Las Cruces

The Colonel from Sixth Army called early in the morning.

"Be sure to do the unit in Las Cruces on the way out to San Francisco and the conference. While you're there, you might as well do the AMSA too." He said.

When any Colonel calls and tells you something like that, there is no other answer but, "Yes sir."

So now we are scheduled to stop in New Mexico on the way to California.

Now the schedule is to fly to El Paso, drive up I-25 to Las Cruces, do the inspection on the truck company in Las Cruces and the AMSA, drive back to El Paso, then fly to San Francisco, get a motel and lunch, drive to the Presidio and be on time for the conference. No big deal. Ha!

The plane left at seven thirty on the dot. It's a direct flight to El Paso. We rented a van at the airport and had a short drive, just about half an hour, up I-25 to The Crosses. On the way up, one of the guys spotted a huge sign that advertised a place called "What-A-Burger" in Las Cruces. None of us had ever heard of What-A-Burger, so we all voted to go there for lunch.

But we had to find the motel first, then the unit and do our standard introductions. By that time everyone said that they were ready for lunch. Now we had to finally find the burger joint. You won't believe those burgers. They should serve them in a washtub. They were huge. And by the way, delicious! The guys and I each got one with fries and a drink.

On the way into town we crossed Colorado Street. The Captain noticed the street names right away and started saying that we should find Maryland Street. Boy what an opening! I just couldn't pass this up, hard as I tried. Look there's Arizona and Nevada, then Utah and California, and we had to stop at a stoplight on Idaho.

I guess I'm more of a sucker for this kind of thing. So I said. "These are all western states. Nobody out here cares about those eastern states." I said.

The two in the back seat almost had a heart attack when I said that. The Captain lit up like an atomic bomb.

"What do you mean nobody cares Blah, Blah, Blah?" He went on for another couple of minutes extolling the virtues of Maryland while the three of us laughed until I had to pull over off the street and park. We sat there and laughed at him until he finally woke up. I wonder how he made Captain.

"You guys thought that was funny didn't you?" He said loudly.

"Yes!" Was our answer.

December in Las Cruces is a nice time of year. We enjoyed ourselves for a couple of days before the San Fran trip.

The truck company in Las Cruces is a big one. There are a lot of trucks and other vehicles. There were bolster trucks, semis, tankers and an assortment of others. Boy I'm glad there's no tracks. We had enough of that a few weeks ago.

We started on the unit right away and all of us worked on each of our specialties to get them started.

Saturday morning the inspection went well. Sometime around the middle of the day, the shop chief told us about the farmer's market downtown. Would we like to go? The Captain was the only one to pipe up and say 'yes'. We all rode with the shop chief and were there in only five minutes.

There was every kind of thing that grows around there and plenty of others available. Since tequila is made from cactus, there was plenty of that for sale too. Both tequila and cactuses. But none of us dared touch any of it. Most of us pieced through for some special candy and things like that, but the Captain said that he and his wife just loved the hot red peppers.

The Captain bought a shock of dried red peppers hanging on one of the booths. I have no interest in any of that stuff. He paid the guy and had him wrap it all in a plastic bag and a paper bag outside it. Then do it all over again.

Rod, Gary and I had no interest in any of the wares today.

The Captain double wrapped the peppers in plastic and heavy paper bags so that he could carry them with him on the plane to San Francisco. None of us had any idea what to say about the plan, so we all voted to shut up.

It's another early direct flight to Los Angeles. Then a short layover, and we arrived at the San Francisco airport at ten thirty. The rental car that I had reserved was waiting for us. Gary got behind the wheel and we're off.

As usual after we got into our motel we all met for lunch at the IHOP across the street. Something smells funny. I wonder what they are cooking here that would smell like that. Oh, well. We should be able to make the conference by noon.

We walked into the conference room at twelve thirty.

A few months ago, after much thought, I tried to do the thing that Mike DiStephano was doing with the loud clothes, but it didn't work. I looked for what he had, but I couldn't find anything just like his suit. So I settled for something I found in a high end men's store in Wichita.

I found a green and white checked three piece suit It's linen and light weight, but very full. It has green leather with the rough side out on the shoulders. This made it look like a western design. I was sure it would work. It did, but not the way I wanted. I thought it might get me the same responses that Mike's clothes got him. I was wrong again.

"Well look here, the team from Wichita have graced us with their presence." Mike De Stefano said.

There's always one in the crowd, and he's always the one.

"You can leave that gaudy linen suit at home next time." Mike said.

Here I was, trying to follow Mike's lead by wearing a bright attention-getting suit, and that's how he treats me. Maybe he's right, it is a little loud.

We had only been there for an hour or so when the General said loudly, "What's that smell?"

We all had noticed it, but none of us were going to say anything about it. We're the out-of-towners!

Several guys walked around the room looking for that smell. Someone found that the smell was our very own Captain. It seems that he had packed the dried peppers into his suitcase for the flight from El Paso. Now all of his clothes smelled really bad.

"Sergeant!" The General said to the Sergeant Major in the back of the room.

When the General yells like that, you jump up and say, "Yes Sir!"

"Take the Captain somewhere and get him cleaned up. And get everything else cleaned up."

Once they had left the room, someone began to laugh. It caught on and soon all of us were laughing.

We didn't see him until we hit Bachelor's bar after the conference let us out.

"I had to buy a new uniform, then drop off all my clothes at a dry cleaners, then back to the room and shower and put on the new uniform and here I am. Good as new. I'll not do that again." The Captain said.

"Did you get rid of the peppers?" Gary asked.

"Not yet." He said.

"Hey Max! Where's the UPS place?"

He gave us directions to the UPS and we immediately picked up that smelly uniform and the peppers and packed and shipped all of it back to his wife. You'd have thought that the Captain would have thought of it himself. But then UPS doesn't take those kind of orders.

Colonel Currie was making his closing remarks when he shocked all of us with a little tidbit. "I have here something for one of our own."

"Mister McAllister, would you please come up here?" He said.

I stood up and slowly moved to the front. I was thinking that this was another one of their off-beat jokes, and I was going to be the butt of it. I looked around to see if there was someone laughing, but didn't see anyone. They all had quizzical looks on their faces.

"I have here a gold bar that General Masters asked me to give you." The Colonel said.

"We don't have a long haired hippie recommended by a General Officer for the position of Warrant Officer very often. But in this case everyone agreed." He said.

He handed me a Warrant's bar and shook my hand.

He took the little gold bar and pinned it on my suit coat and saluted me. I almost fell over. I saluted back and couldn't move. It's a good thing he didn't ask me to speak right then. I don't think I could.

Less than a month later, we were notified that the Captain had been transferred and we would be getting a very senior Major as his replacement. 'Very senior' is an interesting phrase. I hope it's good. We don't need any more tyrants.

I have several days to get a lot done on my car project now. The Holidays provided me a long rest and lots of time to work.

A lot of metal had to be cut away, most of the roof and down to the shelf under the rear window. I removed the side windows and the rear window before. But now all the little pieces of trim and rubber weather stripping and dirt that I missed the first time could be removed. What fun.

The best part of this is that now all the cut edges have to be sanded. I dislike sanding almost as much as a root canal but it has to be done.

I have a dual action sander (DA) for the most difficult sanding jobs on the body or in wood. But it won't handle ragged metal. I bought an inline sander to do finish work with both the metal and the wood parts in case there were any swirls left from the DA. But neither of these will grind the ragged edges of the cut metal down smooth.

My compressor is a little overworked. I might have to replace it. I hope not. I broke down and bought an electric Angle Grinder to finish the metal cuts.

I worked on the car every minute that I had free during the time I was home this time.

I gave the green suit to Goodwill. I can't use it anymore.

Chapter 16

Returning Home

When the conference was over and we were released by the Colonels and the General. I was heading for the motel to get packed and I have a great idea. When we got to the airport, I quietly peeled off from the group and went to the ticket window. I changed my ticket so that I could stop over in Salt Lake for the weekend before I went to Wichita.

I had made the call to my friend there, the girl, not Paul, to tell her when I would be arriving. Audrey said that she would pick me up at the airport.

There is quite a lot of snow on the ground here. Well you would expect that, this is the Rocky Mountains in winter. Just as we had planned, she was standing near the baggage claim section when I arrived. We hugged and kissed until my bag came down the chute.

We hurried to her car and she drove to her house. Once we were inside we talked and played games for hours.

We spent every minute together during the weekend. She especially wanted me to see the huge ski run there called 'Snowbird'. It is really fabulous for a snow skier. But not me. She drove up the skinny winding road clinging to the side wall of the canyon. There really are buildings and people and everything up there. From a distance, it's hard to tell.

The last time I was here, there was sun and nice weather and not a flake to be seen. Today there are mountains of snow everywhere here and skiers are loving it.

Audrey and I had a wonderful weekend. I surprised her and she surprised me. I asked her to marry me.

And she said, "No. But I'll see you anytime you come here, and we'll have lots of fun together."

I don't get it, but that's the way it is. I guess I'll go home and start over.

I picked the original Ford maroon color from the time when the car was being built in order to do it right. I wanted to do the paint and forget it. I had to buy a new paint gun for this special job, mine was old and used up.

When I find a few warm days, it will be time to spray sealer, and primer and finally the color. And sand between each coat to be sure of a mirror finish.

Now that the painting is done I can breathe a little easier. I have parts hanging from every nail, hook and bolt in the garage. That's where they will stay for another trip out of town. I expect that they will dry by then.

Ever since I started this crazy project, I wanted to put wide white walls on the tires. I have been told that tire manufacturers do not make wide white wall tires any more. I would have to get some inserts.

Since the beginning I have searched for these mysterious inserts. Yesterday, Gene showed me a catalog he got in the mail. And in it was an ad for the inserts that I wanted. Gene and I sat down at my desk and made out the order and put it in the mail right then. I can't wait.

Chapter 17

A Major Difference

By the Fourth of July we had pretty much given up any idea that we would be getting another Officer on our team. For that matter, we had given up on getting anyone on our team to replace the Captain.

We had organized the office and all the little things that were needed to keep it going. Rod was back in the Chief's seat and we were all pretty happy about what we were doing.

I always come in a little early and walk out to the shop to have coffee and talk to Dusty and Gene. Then one morning we noticed a big white Ford four door pickup truck drive into the parking lot at the side of the building.

It was on its way to being another hot July day in Kansas. Much like every day in Kansas. The driver appeared not to know exactly where he wanted to park and was hunting for the exact spot. There is only one tree at the edge of the lot and this truck carefully huddled in the shade of that tree.

"That's him!" I said. "They sent us a message that he would be transferred here from Alaska. He must be roasting in that truck about now."

Dusty and I hurried to catch this new guy before he got run over by the people inside.

"Hey! Over here!" I yelled and waved my arms so he would see us.

He looked and turned to walk toward us. He was dressed in civilian clothes and carrying a briefcase. He looked like he was wrung out by the heat.

"Come on inside where it's cool."

We found chairs and coffee and it looked like he would live.

"I'm Tim O'Neil. I'm on the WRAT team." He said.

"So am I. I'm DJ. This is Dusty. He's the shop chief here." I said.

We had been given his name, rank and all the details about his move, so I looked him up in the stud book. He has been a Major for a long time.

"You're the long haired hippie? You don't look like what they described." He said.

"Well, I did get a haircut."

"Oh yes, that must be it." He said and we both laughed.

"They were just having a little fun at our expense. I'll explain it to you later."

The three of us talked till Gene came in and it was time for us all to get to it.

"We'd better go inside and meet the rest of the team."

I introduced him to the guys on the team and we sat around for an hour talking and answering questions. We took a walk down the hall and met the staff. Just like before, everyone smiled, shook his hand and said that they were so glad to see him.

"Look, we set up a desk and chair just for you." I made a production of waving my arm toward the desks in the room.

He laughed with me on that one. We had all four desks set in a square around the office all facing the center, with a visitors chair next to each desk.

For months we have worked on the schedule. We finally got it kind of manageable. But the trip to San Francisco is always a demon in disguise.

I think this Major will bring a whole new look to the team. The Captain wanted to be Lord and Master. This Major will be Team Chief and that's all.

He's kind of happy. It seems like he has humor in his soul. We spent the rest of the week explaining everything we could think of. We made maps, rosters, schedules and reports on everything.

I showed him where the staff meeting is held, and the dates and times of it. And now I don't have to do it anymore. I would like to not wear the uniform during the drills, but General Masters has made it a point to see me at every drill. His comments are always positive, but he still wants to see me in that uniform.

Rod had someone make signs for our door and the desks. We look pretty professional now. I had to laugh, he calls himself Major Disaster. We initially said Major Difference, but it didn't take long to find out he is a major drinker.

Someone from the motor pool at Fort Riley called and said that we should trade in our car for another one. We were driving a nice nearly new feeling Chevy four door that ran good and was easy to drive. But we will go to the Fort and obey their commands like all good soldiers do.

Fort Riley is only about a hundred miles up the road and we haven't been there yet so we will make the trip tomorrow. A short two hour trip in the middle of this country to somewhere we didn't want to be, landed us in Fort Riley Kansas.

The people who called us were gracious enough to supply us with a four door Ambassador Wagon. It didn't take long to find out who got the short end of the stick this time.

"Hey, wait a minute. We seem to be going backwards on this deal."

"No. The car you turned in was an older Chevrolet, and this is a brand new Ambassador wagon with a lot more room for your baggage and books." He said.

Where the car we had was light on its feet and would fly when we wanted to, this Ambassador was long and sluggish, but it had a big back area that would haul all kinds of stuff. The perfect car for a family with more kids than we have.

It was like trading a Corvette for a delivery truck. There was no arguing. We got a lump of crap for a gazelle. Too bad for us.

We finished being screwed by the motor pool at eleven fifteen. Gary said that he thought it was time for lunch. We all looked at our watch and headed for the O Club. I had forgotten this, but every good O Club in the Army has a parking space right in front, next to the door that says "Reserved for any Second Lieutenant."

So, being the rotten no-good hippie that I am, I pulled into the space when we arrived at the club. The Major exploded and we all laughed.

I did finally move the car, but we were all laughing while I did it. The Major finally got the joke and said, "OK, pretty funny, but never again!"

The O Club is always a good place to have a meeting or discuss events and problems. The Major had something on his mind. I could tell. He finally blurted it out.

"All three of you are in the reserves or retired. Why don't you wear the uniform. That bothers me." He asked.

"I'm retired and I don't qualify." Rod said.

"I have way over twenty and I will retire this year, so I didn't see the reason for it." Gary said.

"You know that I'm the 'long haired hippie' and I didn't want to scare the troops." I said. "Besides, I'm AR not RA so it doesn't count."

We all had a good laugh at that and I hope we put it to bed, finally.

Reassembling my new old car after the paint job was a slow process and took days and days. I was in and out twice before I finished the assembly.

Every little piece had to be cleaned, polished, wiped and wiped again and installed. I used all new nuts and bolts and new hardware if I could find it.

Anything I took off that looked worn was replaced. It will be like a new car when I'm done.

Chapter 18

Bismarck Again

Since we really didn't do an inspection in Bismarck when we were there last, we thought we had better go there again and do one. We took a vote and barely decided to go to Bismarck in the good weather part of the year. Actually the vote was the three of us voted no, and the Major voted yes. There is a unit in Minot as well, and we will be taking our life in our hands if there's snow on the ground when we travel to Minot this time.

The last time we went to North Dakota, it was winter, with snow so high you couldn't see over it. Now in July, all the snow is gone and it's tolerable. Almost.

Because we have more experienced heads around this time, we will fly to Denver, change planes and fly to Bismarck. The only driving of any distance will be up Highway 83. It's only a hundred and eleven miles, should be a breeze.

I had reservations at the same hotel as the time before. This time there is no snow on the ground, and we all are glad of that.

We arrived at the Fort Lincoln offices just after noon on Tuesday and flew into the job. Rod and Gary took their magnifying glasses to the motor pool and the Major settled down in the office with the Commander. I had it pretty easy with small arms and electronics.

The unit passed with flying colors and by Thursday we were outbriefing and packing for the drive to Minot.

Minot is only a hundred and eleven miles up the road. It's a major town in North Dakota. There is a large Air Force Base there with planes and everything. That means there will be an O-Club for us to enjoy.

There should be a lot of good places to eat, drink and I'm sure a good motel to stay in. I made reservations at a motel on Highway 2 that looked good to me in the book.

The Major must have a time clock in his head. He timed the drive so that we were walking into the motel at exactly eleven o'clock.

He and the other two ran through the check-in and out to their car and off to a bar for lunch. That means I'm free for the rest of the day.

I decided to go up the hill to the O Club and get some directions to the Army Reserves area. There were only a few people in the place so I sat at the bar.

The bar maid was a gorgeous little dark haired girl. Five foot two or three, thin, great figure and a nice smile. She came out from behind the bar and delivered a tray of drinks to the guys at a table against the far wall.

I got a good look at her and when she walked back to where I was and they did too.

"Hi. What can I do for you?" She said.

"Well the question is what can I do for you, Nicole? I see you're going commando today."

Her name was on a tag pinned to her shirt.

"Yes, but how did Wait a minute. You said 'I see'. What did you see?" She asked.

"The same thing those guys are enjoying right now."

She turned her head toward them. They were all smiling big broad smiles.

"What's going on?" She asked. She was starting to become annoyed.

"I can fix it if you will let me. Turn slowly around so you are facing me and slide back against the bar."

She did what I said.

"Now if you can twist your skirt around to the front and at the same time, you should turn your body around so you face the bar."

She did it very slowly and suddenly she found the problem.

"Oh My God." She said and looked at me in shock. "This has been this way all day. Did you see this?"

"Yes, I did, and I must say that it's one of the most beautiful ones I have seen in a very long time."

"I owe you a big favor. How can I ever repay you?" She said. "By the way, you didn't tell me your name."

"How indeed?"

Suddenly a huge smile came over her and she said. "Where would I find you?"

I showed her my motel key and she smiled and said. "Would about five be good for you? You know you must buy dinner and drinks, don't you?"

"Yes. I'll take care of everything. And I'm DJ."

"I've got to get back to work. See you later, DJ." She said. The smile was still on her face. I like that.

It was time for me to leave, with a smile on my face.

It didn't take long to finish this inspection. There wasn't much equipment for us to look at. It is a small unit and we were done in a couple of hours.

Nicole was very punctual. I heard a knock on my door at five o'clock, and when I opened it, she was standing there smiling from ear to ear.

"You were not very well liked by the guys in the bar this morning." She said. "They were all studying my show and you closed the curtain."

"Well, I did get a little peek before the lights went out."

She stood in the middle of the room.

"Now you get to see the whole show from beginning to end." She opened the curtain and said. "The show must go on." And laughed for almost an hour.

As she was leaving she said that she wanted to move to someplace where it wasn't so cold. I told her that McConnell Air Force Base might be hiring or maybe one of the airplane makers around the town. If she would give me a resume' I would pass it around.

We finished our team work the next day and when I checked out, the clerk gave me an envelope from Nicole. In it was her resume' and a Dear John note. Oh well.

It was a couple of long flights back and I had time to read her note more than once. I'll miss her.

I might as well get this out of the way. I made enough copies of Nicole's resume and set out to distribute them. Cessna and Lear are on the west side of town out by the airport.

Beech is all the way on the east side on Central. As far from each other as you can get. The last two, Boeing and McConnell Air Force Base are on the south side of town. It took me all afternoon to put them all out, but now it's done.

She might not have got all the addresses right, the way they are spread out around town.

I hope Nicole gets some response. She's a good hearted girl, and it doesn't hurt that she is also very good looking. Her resume says she has many talents.

I have had a lot of experience with wood in the past. My dad taught me how to do wood and furniture a very long time ago. Then I took a few furniture making classes from a very good instructor and did very well with it, too. The wood parts won't be difficult, but they will be time consuming. You don't hurry through a furniture project and expect it to be high quality.

I had to build a special table to work on the wood parts of the car body. Each side of the woodie is the same size and shape but the best side of the wood must be on the outside. Each side starts with a four by eight sheet of birch plywood. Then solid pieces of trim are added. I sanded and sanded some more. This is taking months. I thought it would go faster than this.

Chapter 19

Cheyenne

Now that our Captain has been replaced by 'Major Disaster', he said that he likes that name, we can move on with the business we were stationed here to do. It's time to go have some fun, so we are scheduled to go to Cheyenne, Wyoming next.

I am really looking forward to this trip. All the years I have lived in the west, and I never had the chance to visit Wyoming. Although Cheyenne and Casper are the only places that we know Reserve units are located, I am anxious to see the rest of the state.

We may have to take a few trips outside of our normal purview. It's just the middle of fall and the weather is beginning to get cold. The leaves on the trees up here are already falling. But it's not so cold yet that it's uncomfortable. Let's go.

Travel was easy on this one. Fly to Denver, run to the plane and fly to Cheyenne. The Major has said that we should always have two cars so he won't need to wait on someone. I love it. I will be able to investigate interesting places without having someone looking over my shoulder all the time. Besides, I don't care for the night life as much as the others do.

My morning ritual is pretty normal. Up at six, shower, shave, dress, wait for the others, or if I'm really early, go to the coffee shop. I have two eggs, hash browns, toast and coffee. Sometimes bacon, ham or sausage if it's a special. Nothing special for me in the morning, and I'm ready to go.

Rod and Gary both do the same kind of thing. But we have noticed that the Major has a whole different menu. He has two eggs, sunny side up, no hash browns, no toast, no meat, and he doesn't look like he really wants to eat the eggs. He plays with them with the fork until it's time to go, then he eats them, slowly.

Rod must have noticed it too. Later he found me in the arms room of the unit.

"Have you noticed what the Major does when we stop for lunch?" He said.

"No. I didn't pay any attention to him."

"We go to all these fantastic places in these towns and have some of the best food available in the country and he has two or three drafts and that's all." Rod said.

"You know what that means, don't you?" I said.

"Yeah, I do! And it's not good." Rod said.

We didn't say or think any more about it until we broke for the day and went back to the motel. We were staying at a really nice Best Western Motel, and there were free hors d'oeuvres set out in the bar. The Major filled himself a plate and went to the bar and came back with two bottles of beer.

"I like this place." He said. "There is free food and two-fers on the bar."

Well, that answers all of Rod's questions.

After we finished for the day in the unit, Rod and I drove down to the train yard and walked around. Man, is that thing big! We looked at everything that we could. I wish I had brought a camera with me, but I didn't.

As we were driving back to the motel, Rod spotted another big railroad steam engine in a park. He was in a hurry and I only caught a glimpse of it as we sped by, but it was a huge one too. It looked bigger than anything we had seen at the yard.

One more day here. We went to every bar and hangout. We even went to the 'Green Door'. Lots of good food and drink at every stop. The Major likes the night life, but I can't take it. I don't know how he does it.

The drive to Casper is up I-25 a hundred and eighty miles. We found another great motel and the Major was very content. Casper is considerably smaller than Cheyenne, but It's a growing town. We found several fun things to do.

I don't like to go to a bar for lunch, the others don't seem to mind. I walked out to the street and saw someone with a taco in her hand.

"Where did you get a taco?" I asked.

She pointed to a little hole in the wall across the street. I ran there and bought a taco and some lemonade.

I found a seat and relaxed for a few minutes with my big Mexican sandwich. It was great.

"Hi. You're not from around here, are you?" She asked.

"No. Here on business."

"I'm Lisa, who are you?"

"My name is DJ."

"That's not a name. Those are initials." She said.

"Sorry, best I can do."

"What kind of work do you do?" She asked.

"I work for the Government."

"I work at the clothing store right there." She pointed across the street to the store.

"Well Lisa, I've finished my taco and I have to get to work."

"Would you like to have dinner with me tonight after we get off work?" She said. "I know a really good place not far from here?"

"You're asking me to have dinner with you?" I'm sure there was surprise in my voice.

"Yes, I am." She said.

"I would love to." I said. "Where will I pick you up?"

"I will pick you up. Where are you staying?" She asked.

I told her the motel and the room that I was in. She arrived at five thirty and was dressed very nice. The dress looked pretty thin and it was blowing in the breeze. She's about five foot six, a little more in heels, small built and very pretty. We went to a restaurant she knew in the center of town that had the best steaks. After the meal we walked around town and talked. We arrived back at the motel about seven thirty.

"Would you like to come in?" I asked.

"Maybe just for a minute." She said.

The phone rang at six am and I picked it up. "Your wake up call." Someone said and hung up.

I was already awake and so was she. "Well, it looks like it's time to shower and go to work again." I said.

"Yes, but I'm going to feel a lot better at work today. Thanks for everything, and call me the next time you're in Casper or Cheyenne." She said.

Lisa and I were already having breakfast when the guys strolled into the coffee shop. We did our greetings, finished eating and left for Cheyenne.

This whole thing was like a rerun of a movie I had seen before where the characters were the same, but with different actors playing them.

Why can't I find a girlfriend in Wichita?

"Hey DJ. What happened to you last night? We looked all over for you." Rod said.

"Oh, I just saw a movie I had seen once before. That's all." I said. "It's one I realy enjoyed before, and I really enjoyed it again." They probably noticed my smile.

Rod said he was able to get into the Major's room this morning and wait for him to get ready. He noticed that he had two cans of beer sitting on the air conditioner all night.

The Major told him that in the morning before he comes down for breakfast, he drinks them to start the day. Rod also found out that he drinks two six packs of beer every day. I know I couldn't possibly do that.

We finished our work and drove back to Cheyenne. The next morning we were on a plane to Denver then another to Wichita. Then drive home and collapse on the bed again.

When we all arrived in the office the next day, Gary announced that he would be retiring soon. He had already been to CPO and filled out all the paper-work.

Gary will be turning sixty in about a month. His last days are already started. The major notified Sixth Army and they will get started looking for a replacement. I made a special trip out to the shop to tell Gene to apply for the job. No, I insisted that he apply. He is a very knowledgeable mechanic and I would like to have him with us.

This is not a great job, but there will be those who will apply for it.

We interviewed four men for the job. I wrote a rec-ommendation for Gene. The Major and the other two wrote their recommendations, but I didn't see them. We waited almost a month after the interviews were completed and sent in before we heard a word from them.

The good news was that they did hire Gene, and he will start in two weeks.

Back to work on the car project. I'm getting it done, but it's a lot of work and sometimes very hard work.

Now comes the hard part, I mean the wood part. I was lucky enough to find a set of plans already drawn up for the wood parts by another company in California. The drawings could be transferred to wood and plywood to make the parts for the sides and then for the roof and the rear door.

A few years ago, I took a few furniture making classes from a very good instructor and did very well with it. I hope I can do a job that the instructor would be proud of. The wood parts won't be difficult, but they will be time consuming. You don't hurry through a furniture project and expect it to be high quality.

Chapter 20

Omaha

We worked in the office and finished all the subservient tasks. Then we went to each of the units located right there in our building. Might as well get them out of the way and teach the Major what we do both at the same time.

Everyone seems to be settled after our last trip to San Francisco, so we'll begin another round of "friendly" visits to the folks in the real world.

Omaha is one of the towns I like to visit. There are so many things to do and places to go. There is Aksarben Park. That's Nebraska spelled backwards. This is a must see place. There is Fort Omaha on the north side. We have a unit there, so I get to see it every time we visit.

We don't know how the Major will react to all the great restaurants and other attractions, but I guess we'll wait and see.

Near the Fort is an unbelievable restaurant called Mr.C's. Christmas lights all around the inside and the best prime rib in the world. A special on prime rib sandwiches at lunch. But there's more.

Of course everybody knows that Godfathers Pizza originated here. We always visit there when we can. I always eat too much pizza, I'm sure I will this time too.

But tonight we are having dinner at the Bohemian Girl Restaurant down on Thirteenth Street. I have been there before. There are photos of famous people and presidents who had patronized the restaurant on the walls all around the place. I remember seeing a photo of Elvis once.

That's the place where you go across a bridge that has an off-ramp in the middle of it. I had never seen one like that before and probably will never see another.

One funny thing about it that I remember, was all the choices of entrees and side dishes there were. We all wanted to see what would happen when it was time for Gene to order. The waitress came with menus and three of us knew just what we wanted after a quick look. Rod was first.

"Are you ready to order? She asked Rod.

"Yes. I am. I would like the Jaeger Schnitzel, please. I have always enjoyed Veal and the wine sauce and mushrooms they add here are a real delicacy." He said.

The waitress started with the question and answer period but Rod stopped her in the middle.

"I would like the Czech Dumpling, broccoli, sauerkraut, no bread and coffee. Thank you."

The Major was next. He ordered Svicova. I didn't know what that is but he did.

"It's Czech style Sauer Braten and it's delicious." He said.

The waitress started through the list and he ordered whipped potatoes, liver dumpling, broccoli, no kraut, rye bread and iced tea. That's the most food I've ever seen or heard him order yet.

"What would you like to drink, sir? Coffee, tea or beer?"

We all knew the answer to that question, but wait for it.

"We have a fine Czech imported beer on tap called Pilsen Urquell. It comes in a large chilled mug." She said.

"You read my mind, that beer will be just fine." He said.

The waitress turned to me.

Now it's my turn. "I would like the Hassenpheffer, please."

My dad raised rabbits when I was in school. I didn't get involved much in it. What I did know was that baked or roasted, or whatever the cook does to it, it was delicious. I have never been to another restaurant that served rabbit. I'm making the most of it.

I didn't get my choices made as quick as the others and the waitress began the list.

"Dumpling or potato?" She said.

"Potato."

"Baked or mashed?"

"Mashed."

"Broccoli or peas?"

"Broccoli."

"Sauerkraut or Czech cabbage?"

"Neither."

"Rye or white bread?"

"Rye and coffee."

Last on the list was Gene. He was looking at the menu and reading the words out loud in a low voice. I was sure he had never seen any of this kind of food.

"Now sir, have you made your choice?" She said.

"I'm new at this, but I would like to try the duckling, please." He said.

"Yes sir. I'll go slow for you." She was smiling.

"Dumpling or potato?"

"Potato."

"Baked or mashed?"

"Baked."

"Broccoli or peas?"

"Peas."

"Sauerkraut or Czech cabbage?"

"Sauerkraut."

"Coffee, tea or beer?"

"Tea, please."

We all had a good laugh at Gene and his handling of the Q and A period.

The food was outstanding. The Major had another large chilled mug of the imported beer and seemed to be very calmed down after he drank it. Maybe this is the way he gets when the alcohol affects him.

We ate and we talked and we ate and we talked. Soon the waitress was back for us.

"What would you like for dessert gentlemen?" She said.

I hadn't even thought of it. "What do you have tonight?"

"Apple strudel or Kolacky." She said.

Of course the Major didn't order anything, but Rod had the Strudel and Gene and I had the Kolacky. As with everything else, it was fabulous.

We have been to the zoo, President Ford's house, we saw the Big Boy engine at the railroad yard and a lot of unique stores and shopping areas. This is our last night here, tomorrow we move on to Fremont and another unit.

We are going to eat at a place called Grandmother's on Eighty Fourth and L tonight. It is supposed to be special, and we are always up for something special. Well, whoever told us about this place was right. They nailed it! The food was terrific, the drinks were good and the price was right. That's three for three.

We left town early in the morning and drove up Highway 77 to Fremont. The Colonel in DCSLOG told us to "make sure you look at this one very closely." He didn't say why and you don't question a full bull when he issues an order. I'm not as dumb as I look.

On the way up, because of the dark skies, we made a side trip to a town called Wahoo. Any town with a name like that deserves a stop if only for a minute. We drove through town. It's a small town just like you would expect a town with that name in the middle of Nebraska would be.

On the drive up from Wahoo, we noticed that the sky got darker and darker behind us. I'm not from the Midwest, so I don't know how to read the weather signs, but this did not look good.

When we arrived in Fremont, they told us that a tornado ran through Omaha just about where we were the day and night before. The storm came right through that part of town and took out more than a few buildings.

The unit is small and it should have taken a small amount of time, but with all the concern about the severe weather, it took us all day. Besides, we didn't want to drive back to Tornado Alley while there was one of those monsters lurking around.

They had the TV news on and there were a lot of photos of places that we recognized.

This is the unit that lost the radioactive source for the radiacmeter. DCSLOG was very incensed about it. They hadn't found it by the time we were there. Neither did we.

We were trying to do the inspection and keep an eye on the television coverage of the storm. Most of the things the unit owned that we looked at today were in good condition and only needed some small maintenance.

I gave the armorer some tips on how to best maintain the weapons.

The TV station showed a group of buildings at Seventy Second and Dodge Streets. It was huge. It took up the whole block. It had white roofs and looked like someone flattened the whole block with their foot.

It turned out that there was a bar, a restaurant and a dance hall under all those roofs. I hope it was empty.

One guy said that a restaurant located at Eighty Fourth and L Street was severely damaged. That's where we had dinner last night! That's too scary for me.

There are photos of a Bakers Grocery store on Seventy Second that was badly damaged. These tornados are not friendly and I'm ready to go back to the mountains.

Boy, am I glad that trip is over. Tornados are the most destructive kind of storms there is, I think. And I don't want to be around them at all.

I have a week off and I'm going to immerse myself in the car and try to forget the tornado that could have got us.

The wood for the sides and roof are mostly done, but it has taken a lot longer than I expected. One thing I know, persistence always wins out. I just keep on keeping on. I'm measuring, marking, cutting, sanding and fitting each piece of wood one at a time.

The wood won't make it run any better, but it sure will make it look good. I hope.

Chapter 21

Lincoln

Lincoln is the capital of Nebraska and is about a hundred miles west of Omaha on the Interstate. It's a city of about three hundred thousand. Not some little hamlet. It also houses the University of Nebraska. Go Big Red!

There is a Brigade located there. Makes sense, big town, lots of people, big unit. Lots of equipment. Lots of work for us.

In the morning it's always the same for me. This morning held a surprise that I had never seen before. After all the cleanup, and dressing I need to do, I stepped out on the balcony to see everyone dressed in red. It's football season.

There were women in red dresses, skirts, coats, shirts, shoes, hats and gloves. Men in everything red right down to the socks, even football jerseys. The Nebraska Huskers are the University of Nebraska's college football team. The team color is red. So 'Go Big Red'! This is the local cry. And I heard it ten thousand times this morning.

They were a little noisy but not so much that it would wake anyone. Probably everyone in the motel was dressed in red and outside already.

As I was making my way through the red sea, Rod grabbed me and we ran for the coffee shop. We found a booth in back and ordered before the others found us. The Major was laughing about the red sea. It's the first time I saw him laugh for real since he's been here. Maybe there's hope for him after all.

The Major did the inbriefing and we were off and running. Their building was so clean that it surprised me. I have been around Army people for many years and I never have seen things so clean. I accidentally walked into a back room to find two guys in fatigues with mops and brooms and rags washing the walls and floor.

I could not find even one thing wrong that I could write about. That's totally unfair. It looks like we weren't even here. I need to write something. It's too bad the rest of the Arcom isn't as good as this place. I worked extra hard to find anything that I could write up. No dice.

There was either a heavy dew or a light rain last night, and there were guys outside wiping it off of the vehicles. Now that is conscientious.

We didn't see the big game, but we saw a lot of folks in town sporting red clothes. Every piece of clothing you can think of in red.

Rod knew of a great place on L Street with the best steaks. We all enjoyed them for lunch. We took our time with lunch. The Brigade didn't need us now anyway.

I bought a house in Wichita a while ago. I would like to try my hand at making some good red wine in the basement. When I was just a teenager, my dad took me with him when we went for lunch with a friend named Joe Frank. He was Italian and very proud of it.

He made a beautiful dark red wine that was sweet and didn't have much of a bite to it. He called it Mogen David, but I know the real name for it.

I had never drank anything like that and I asked him if he would show me how to make it. To my surprise he agreed and told me the most unusual recipe for making wine I have ever heard. I wrote it down as he dictated it. I didn't want to miss a single word.

I didn't have a place to do this before, but now I do and I need bottles. Green bottles. A guy in the unit told me about a liquor store where I might find what I want. The two of us drove there and he told the owner what we wanted.

"Sure thing. I'll be glad to get you some wine bottles. Could you take two cases?" He asked.

"Be glad to, thanks."

We pretended to be bearing down on the Brigade for the rest of the weekend, but we had already looked at everything twice and sometimes three times and couldn't even find chingle marks on the nuts and bolts

Sunday afternoon we finished everything and packed up to leave in the morning. It's a couple hundred miles to Wichita, but we can be there by noon, maybe. I might have some time to do finish work on the new car.

I finally got all the wood finished and installed on the woodie. The car looks like a car now. I had to stain and polyurethane all the wood before it was assembled. That took most of a week, but that was the easy part. Now to get the car to run!

Maybe the hardest part of the woodwork was making air vents to direct the air across the motor for cooling. I had to make special ports on the sides of the body with a fan to pull the air in and make it flow across the motor and out the rear door. And I didn't want them to be very obvious. I actually tried to make them unseen.

Just about the time Gene and I had this part all done, it was time to go out on another trip again.

I took a big chance when I found a wrecked Porsche 356A across town, and brought it home on a trailer. It was hit head-on. Everything in the front end was demolished, but the motor and tranny was not hurt, I hope.

Chapter 22

Topeka

Topeka is only a hundred and forty miles up Interstate 35 from Wichita. A good three hour drive. But of course, we had to stop some place for coffee and eggs. It's a rule. You can't drive a trip like this in the morning without breakfast. We arrived at the city line at eleven o'clock. We knew the unit would be breaking for lunch, so we took our time getting to the motel and a bite to eat.

We walked in to the Reserve Center right after lunch and were greeted by several officers, one of which was the IG. This IG is a Major Pain and he jumped on Tim at the first opening. All the MASH Officers stood around with their mouths open wondering "what is this guy's problem?"

He went into a big loud spiel about "You are not supposed to be here." Tim yelled at him to shut up and he would call Sixth Army and the IG Major Pain could talk to them himself.

Tim said. "I will abide by whatever they say."

It seems that our Major Difference was right, and everyone there could see it on the IG's face loud and clear. But the IG did not leave. Instead he hung around like a bad cold and harassed everyone. The MASH people got pretty tired of him and his one cohort, sorry, assistant.

One good thing was that there were only two of them and four of us. That gave each of us a little breathing room.

What we have this weekend is a good old fashioned MASH unit. Lots of beautiful girls, doctors, nurses and officers. The Major gave his standard inbriefing and answered all their questions. Strangely enough, the IG had no comments during the inbrief.

I headed for the arms room. I wanted to get it out of the way as soon as I could. One thing that you can be sure of is this. A MASH unit knows the word 'clean'. There will not be any discrepancies for something not being clean. I guarantee it. Just as I finished the weapons, I was stopped by an old friend of mine.

I know one of the nurses in the MASH in Topeka. She was at the Arcom when I first arrived and helped me with some of the problems that I had. Since she was an officer, she was a big help with the little problem about the long hair. Nancy is probably a Major by now. She was an experienced nurse and very caring of others.

Nancy is married and has two kids who adore her. Most of the Arcom knows her from her work in the local Wichita hospital.

Nancy has always tried to get me fixed up with one of her friends or nurses. Now I'm a captive in the Reserve Center I know that she is going to make the most of it.

The first girl she introduced me to was Shirley. Shirley is a Lieutenant who works at the hospital in Topeka. She is as beautiful as all of the others, but she lives two hundred miles from me when I'm home.

We spoke for a few minutes, shook hands and she was off to her job.

"Here comes a girl from Wichita, DJ. I'm sure you will like her." She said.

"DJ, I would like to introduce you to Angela Foster. Angie, meet DJ." She said. "She hasn't finished her degree work, so she is still enlisted scum like you, DJ."

Nancy and Angela both got a big laugh out of that. Neither of them know about the Warrant bar. I'm not advertising it.

Angie extended her hand to me and I took it and held it for a short time. She felt soft and smooth and confident. I liked the feel. She smiled and only pulled her hand away when Nancy said something. I think I like this girl and would like to talk to her.

"Are you busy right now, Angie? Maybe we could talk for a few minutes before you have to get back to the old grind?"

"Sure." She said. "Let's go outside where everyone can't hear us."

"We're going to be here for the weekend. Would you like to have dinner with me tonight?" I asked.

"That is just what I was thinking. What time are you finished here?" She asked.

"I could go now. I'm all done except for the IG and writing up my part of the report."

"Great! So am I. Let's sneak out now." She said.

"I'll have to tell Rod so they won't go looking for me. But he will keep it to himself."

"OK. I'll meet you out front at my car. It's the blue Triumph." She said.

I found Rod and whispered to him what we were doing. He smiled and nodded his head 'OK' and I hot-footed out to her car. She had the car running and the passenger door open. I guess that's an invitation.

She drove to her motel and we went inside and she poured a little drink for us. We sat and talked for at least an hour about everything. The Reserves, her family, my family, our team, Wichita, the hospitals there, her car, my car, and on and on.

Finally she got up and said. "Did you want to go eat now?"

"Whenever you want. I'm ready when you are."

She stood up and began to change her clothes right there in front of me. When she was half done, she stopped and smiled to herself and said to me. "You know, maybe there is something you can do for me."

Later we went to Howard Johnson's for the shrimp. They serve a really good meal, whether you order the shrimp meal or not. We both ate too much but we'll survive. She dropped me off at my room and I took the rest of the day off. I'll see her tomorrow.

The next day, the drill was in full swing and everyone was moving in all directions. One by one, I talked to as many of the members as I could. Most of them like the MASH and enjoy helping anyone they can.

Angie came by and only stopped to say. "Dinner tonight, DJ?"

"Sure, if you want."

"OK. Your turn to drive. See you later." She said.

We went to Church's Chicken and even though it's a fast food place, it was some of the best chicken I have ever had. She wanted to show me the State Capitol Building. We walked all though it and she told me all about the building, the town and the state. Now I am authority on Kansas.

We are a funny bunch. Rod and Gene would rather find the best restaurants with the most unusual food. The Major would rather have two-fers and hors d'oeuvres. And I would rather be by myself or go out with someone for some fun.

I picked up Angie at five and she told me about one of her favorite places. The food was fabulous and the price was right. Again we spent most of our time talking about anything that popped into our head.

I had to help her into her room. She tripped on something today and hurt her leg. I rubbed her leg for a while and got the blood flowing and the pain began to slow down.

The next day we saw all the vehicles and all the medical equipment and tools. I had no idea there was this much. I watched every episode of "MASH" on TV, this was all different.

I saw Angie later that afternoon. She asked me if I danced. I told her that I was terrible at it but I could stand in the middle of the floor and fake it. She laughed and said to pick her up at five.

Later Angie told me that she had a boyfriend in Wichita and that we probably wouldn't see much of each other anymore. I'll see her once in a while, but only to wave hello.

We finally got the report all done and the Major did a fine job of outbriefing it and we left for Wichita Monday morning.

I feel certain that the Major Pain IG will say all kinds of bad things about us. But it's done now and who cares?

I stripped any parts from the wrecked Porsche that didn't get damaged from the wreck, for backup parts. I'll keep them here in a drawer and on a shelf in case I need something.

We will add the Porsche engine and transaxle from that old car to my masterpiece. Gene agreed to do most of the work when we get back.

I was supposed to be the grunt for him. It didn't take as long as I thought it would. He said that it bolted right in like it was an original part of the car. Gene knows more about VW and Porsche than most of the people in this town. I have found a very good friend.

Time out for another out-of-towner. This one was only ten days long. But I got back to work the next day after we arrived home.

Chapter 23

A Little Fun

Gene and I go to a lot of different places together. He knows all the best places to go for fun in this town. I'm only along for the ride.

"Hey DJ, do you know how to bowl?" He said.

"Yeah. I used to set pins in a bowling alley when I was in high school."

"You any good?" He asked.

"Not bad, I guess. I can roll a two hundred every once in a while."

"Let's go do it. I'd like to see this." He said.

"What? You mean now?"

"Sure! Why not?" He said.

"OK, then."

Gene knows where everything is located in the town. I just live here. We drove to the Bowling Center, (note the capital letters) and said we'd give it a try. After spending a great deal of time looking around the place, we rented shoes and found a big black ball with holes drilled in it that almost fit my hand.

We threw three lines and each one was a little better than the last. It's only been since I was fifteen or sixteen that I did this last. I made a fair showing, one thirty nine, one fifty six and one seventy three. I can still throw that little hook, but I need a lot of practice.

Gene did a lot better than I did with one fifty eight, one seventy five, and a five strike run to one ninety one. Show off!

The next place was a bar with a couple of dart boards. Gene can really hit the target with those darts. I took the darts and threw all three at the target, but only one hit the board, and it wasn't in the center. It was barely on the board.

"I could do a lot better if I could shoot the target with my gun." I said.

The bar almost cleared out with that comment.

The bartender was down on the floor behind the bar, and most of the patrons were up and ready to run.

"Wait. I'm not going to shoot anything or anybody. I just can't throw these things, but I'm in the Army and I've been taught how to handle weapons of all kinds. Darts aren't one of them."

There was a sigh of relief in the building and everyone found their seats again.

Of course, Gene was standing there laughing the whole time.

It was time to leave and find a more hospitable place to be stupid in.

"You were talking about shooting. We could go to a range and pick off the tin cans and the paper targets." Gene said.

I thought that was a good idea, but as we were driving along, I saw a bunch of flyers taped in a grocery store window.

"Wait! Stop! There's a bunch of flyers in that window there."

Gene stopped and I ran back to read them.

A flea market in a park, a flea market and a gun show inside a big building, An RV Show at the Civic Center. The Baseball team is playing soon, a NASCAR race at 81 Speedway and something on the Zoo. Gene parked and came back to read them with me.

"Whaddaya think? Any of this look good to you?" Gene asked.

"Yeah. Let's go to the outdoor flea market first. I'm looking for a swing and some stuff for my back yard. Then you pick the next one. I want to build some kind of kitchen or place to eat and relax in the back yard."

We found the park and walked around for an hour or so. I had a big fancy hot dog and some strawberry lemonade from The Dawg House. I was terrific! I found a few things that would work for my yard. We talked to the sellers and made a deal with them to deliver the stuff tomorrow afternoon.

Gene wanted to go to the gun show. Good thing he was driving. I didn't know where it was.

The gun show was in a building in old shopping center. It's big enough to be a good grocery store.

We looked at all the pistols and rifles for a long time. I saw a couple I would like to have but the prices were too high for me right now. I have several guns at home and I always keep my James Bond close to me.

Besides, I just spent most of my money on the swing and stuff for the back yard.

As we were walking out, Gene said, "Let's go to the – - Hey, look at this!"

He picked up a pistol off of a table and showed it to me.

"I've been looking for one of these for a long time." He said.

He handled it and examined it for a couple minutes and asked the seller what the price was. The price must have been right, because he took out his wallet and made a deal for it right then. We were going to go to the RV and Home Show I thought, but not with him carrying a gun.

"My house is close, if you want to leave it there with mine for the day."

"Yeah! Let's do that and then go watch the race. Eighty One Speedway is up north of town, and I don't want any attention because of this." He said.

It's a long drive to the racetrack and wouldn't you know it? It was deserted! The race was last week. Neither one of us caught that little fact on the flyers.

"You wanna go to the RV show?"

"Sure. Let's go." He said.

The RV and Home show was in the Civic Center. I think I have seen it, maybe I could find it, maybe not. Gene drove right there and we hurried in. I never thought I wanted an RV, so I put on my 'Interested buyer' face and we were in the right place. We looked at several of them. We climbed into the first one, it looked nice until I heard the price.

All of a sudden my face changed to my 'Let's go look at something I can afford' face.

There were all kinds of things for the house and gardens, but I'm still trying to get my cars and garage finished.

It was still early and Gene asked if I would like to see some of the planes they fly in and out of McConnell.

So off we went to the Air Base. We found a good place on the Boeing side outside the base and sat in the car. It wasn't long before we saw an A-10. It's a two engine plane that flies low to the ground and provides support for troops. It was painted Army green. I think that's why Gene likes it.

During the time we sat there we saw KC-135 Tankers, F-4 Fighters, F-16 Fighters and a Boeing 727 painted in the strangest looking green. There's a lot of planes flying around, I wonder what's going on. We were there well after dark, close to midnight.

It was a long day and I was glad to get to my bed.

Now that the Porsche motor is in the woodie and it is tuned up, Gene says that this car should run over a hundred miles per hour.

Gene did a test drive and came back ten minutes later with some bad news. "You have got to put some brakes on this thing. Now that we put the new motor in it, there's so much power that it won't stop."

"The regular drum brakes that come on this thing are way too small. The Karmann Ghia has disk brakes. We'll have to make a big change." He said.

We spent the rest of the week finding, buying and installing a set of disk brakes from an old Ghia that Gene found in a salvage yard. More cleaning, polishing, painting, unbolting and bolting. What fun! Now that the car is done, again, I am sure that Gene will test it to the max, and a hundred will be on his schedule.

I added a new twelve volt alternator, battery and all new lights. I want the other drivers to see me coming, and going.

Chapter 24

Leavenworth

Leavenworth is a word that everyone in this country either knows or should know. The word is scary enough just by itself. But when you are standing in front of the real thing, it is a lot more than you can imagine. And the rest of the Team wants to go inside. You must be kidding! NO! Not Me! I'll stay outside! The people inside might like me too much!

There is a little Engineer Detachment across the street. The other three guys were just drooling to get a look at anything inside Leavenworth. I told them that they did not want to go in there, because the door opens 'in' only. There's no getting out. They didn't believe me, but they didn't go inside.

It's winter here and there is snow on the ground and the cold will give you chills. But that is warm compared to the feeling I get about the thought of being inside there for the rest of my life. Just looking at the outside of this place gives me chills.

I can't even imagine what it would be like to be inside this concrete and granite monolith. I'll stay outside. I said that before. Sorry. If you haven't been here, you don't know what you're missing. Maybe you don't want to see this either.

I finally convinced the gun-ho clowns on the team that they and I did not want to go into that place. I can't even call it a building. It's a monstrous looking place. We retreated to the little Engineer Detachment. To my surprise the detachment had enough tools in their meeting room and the storage rooms for a crew of men to build a house without looking for the right tool.

All the tools were laid out on the floor around the inside walls of the little building they had. It looked like a home show at the mall.

There were hammers, crowbars, wrenches of every kind, levels, tape measures, hatchets, axes, saws, and any other carpentry tool you might need.

There were trowels, floats, tuck pointers, a bull float, even a screed. I always use a two by four. It would take me an hour to tell you about all the tools and their uses.

Every tool was clean. Not just clean, but wiped clean! Not one bit of grease or dirt on any of them.

There were no vehicles, and only a few small arms. There were books of every kind and description telling how to build, teardown, and everything in between. The only item the Engineer Detachment was missing was an architect.

The next day was a lazy day for us until all hell broke loose. Nicole walked through the door and said. "DJ!" In a loud voice and I jumped at the noise she made. She came to my desk and I stood as she hugged me. There was a girl about the same age as Nicole with her, but Nicole didn't introduce her. She sat on the chair at my desk and smiled at me.

All three of them had their eyes wide open and staring at the dark haired beauty hugging me. I could see that introductions were in order, but I was hesitant about how to handle it. So I did a comedy routine and let the guys take it from there.

"This is the Major. He is a hundred and has a hundred kids and grandkids."

"This is Rod. He is only seventy five and has seventy five grand kids."

"This is Gene. He is single but really ugly and far too old for you. Nice group that I work with huh?"

Nicole immediately went to Gene and offered her hand and when he extended his hand she hugged him and put a little kiss on his cheek.

Gene's face lit up with a smile from ear to ear.

"This is Nicole. I met her at the O Club in Minot. She was showing off as the barmaid there." I laughed as I said it.

She giggled a little and began to tell us why she was here.

"I came to tell you that I landed a job with Cessna as a clerk. And the pay is far better than I was getting back home. I sure appreciate what you did for me." She said.

"What did you do to her, DJ?" Rod said.

"Not to me, but for me. I gave him some resume's and he passed them out to employers. I couldn't have done that. And I love the warm weather here." She said.

I sat and offered my hand to Nicole's girlfriend. Her hand was small and warm, not with heat, but with friendship. I could feel it.

"I'm DJ. I'm glad to meet you."

"Oh, I'm Karen. I know who you are. Nicole told me ALL about you. That's why I'm here." She said.

"My, would you look at the time! It's time for lunch. Are you hungry Karen?"

"Yes, I am very hungry right now." She said.

"Let's go!"

"If you think it's warm now, wait for summer. It really gets hot here." Gene said.

She sat on Genes lap and said. "Will you keep me warm till then?"

We were both smiling as we walked out when the discussion was still going on.

Gene is smiling now and not saying a word. It looks like he has a new girlfriend.

After this trip, I was glad to get home and test drive my new car. I was looking forward to that. Gene was too.

My pretty little car is finally turning out to be a pretty little car for real. It's about time. I have put in months and dollars on this little project, and it finally looks like I can see the end of it.

The last thing to do on the car was the upholstery. I bought seats from a Honda Accord, but I'm going to have Mike Tabor do the finish work on them. I don't know the first thing about that business. I didn't think I could even be of any help to him. I asked if I could help and he said no. I don't have any background in it, so I don't feel bad about that.

Just about the time he had this part all done, it was time to go out on another trip again. Mike guaranteed me that the car would be done when I came back for it.

Chapter 25

Olathe

Olathe, Kansas is on the southwest edge of Kansas City. It is a prosperous part of the KC Metro district. The town is filled with nice expensive homes. There are well maintained streets and parks. There are a lot of stores and small businesses. There is at least one very nice shopping center.

Olathe looks like the kind of town you would be proud to say was your hometown.

Olathe is also the home of the only aviation unit in the Arcom. And these guys have a reputation that they really know their business.

We have been directed, that is, ordered, to inspect every unit in every Arcom at least once. This is their once.

None of us have any knowledge of air vehicles. I understand the avionics, but that's the easy stuff.

Those things sitting outside on that big patch of concrete are helicopters. CH-47 helicopters. Not some little one seater that the radio stations fly and pretend to give you the news and weather as they fly around the city.

The CH-47 is a dual rotor hauling machine. I have seen them pick up some very heavy loads and take them away.

None of us know how to inspect airplanes, especially these airplanes. But their records, publications, small arms, tools and vehicles were all good. There was even a fifty cal in the arms room. I didn't try it, but I'm sure it will fire. There are times that you should leave well enough alone. It had a firing pin in the safe and everything. And the ammo was safely put away in the safe for that purpose.

We got done early with our piece of the inspection and were sitting in the boss's office. He's a long time Chief Warrant Officer and runs the whole operation very well. As I went through my part of the inspection, I asked the men how well the whole place was doing. Each one said it was a great place to work.

"So you're the 'long haired hippie'. I hear General Masters really got you, but you bounced back. How did you do it?" He said.

"I only did what he told me. The thing about the hair was pretty obvious, but I had only been moving to the new job and in town only two days and barbers aren't open on Sunday or Monday. I didn't even know where I was going."

"I heard that he made you a Warrant." He said.

"It certainly wasn't anything that I did. I don't know how it happened. The Colonel at Sixth Army pinned it on and saluted me and I almost fell over."

The guys on the team laughed a lot at that. They were there when it happened.

"Where's your uniform?" He asked.

"I don't wear it. I'm only a reservist."

"I sure would like to see you in uniform tomorrow. The General is curious to find out if he made a good decision." He said.

"It's in our car, but it's probably wrinkled."

"We have an iron if you know how to use it." There was a group chuckle there. "I can even recommend a cleaner who will get it ready for you." He was smiling now and enjoying this just a little too much. So was the Major and the other two.

"We're done here for today. I'll be glad to take you to the cleaners to get everything ready." The Major said. Now he's smiling and about to bust.

The Major drove to the place that Graves told us about. The cleaner said that he could get it ready in ten or fifteen minutes. I decided to wait on it. They didn't want to sit around in a dry cleaners shop while we waited on my uniform, but I wasn't going to let these guys drag me down again.

I came to work the next morning with my freshly cleaned and pressed uniform with my fancy little gold bar and my scant few medals that make up the rainbow. The enlisted guys in the unit didn't know who I was but they did what was expected of them. They saluted. There was some talk around as I walked into the hangar and back to the office.

Mister Graves, the Chief Warrant, also had his uniform on and met me at the door to his office.

"Well, good morning Mister McAllister. It's nice to see you could make it today." He said. He was smiling and almost laughing when he said it. He has medals that almost cover his chest.

He carefully examined my medals and said. "I see you have a very important ribbon here." He pointed to one in particular.

"That's my ribbon for being stupid. I zigged when I should have zagged."

We all went into the office and sat and Graves picked up the phone and made a call.

"Good morning, Sir. This is Mr. Graves in Olathe. You asked me to call and tell you the results. It appears that your long haired hippie has made an amazing recovery and may at sometime in the future become a real US Army soldier." Then he laughed and said. "Yes sir, I think you are right. Thank you, sir."

"The man on the other end thinks that he may have made a good choice, after all. Now that you have a haircut and a clean uniform." He said.

I could tell he wanted to laugh, but he held it in. But there was a large smile plastered on his face most of the day.

Everyone in the room laughed for several minutes and razzed me at the same time.

The Major did the outbrief and we got out of there. I was running to the car. We're going back to our office, so I don't have to drive. I found the back seat and hunkered down.

At least I got out of that uniform at the motel before we started back. I felt relieved that it was over for now at least. I know it will come up again. The Major loved it and Rod and Gene are both ready to laugh out loud.

As soon as I got back, I made sure that uniform was hung up in the closet with the plastic covering it. I don't want to go through this again.

The worst part of this whole game is this. The General will be expecting to see me in that uniform during their drills every Monday night from now on.

With a lot of help from Gene, I finished the car about three months ago. He did almost all the work on the rebuild of the engine, and the installation. I picked up, lifted, held, hunted for, found and did anything else I could do for him.

He did all the fine adjustments and it runs like a new car. That little thing with the liquid and the bubble in it that he sat on top of the carburetors was the most interesting and the most beneficial of all the tools he had, but the hardest part was the transaxle.

I have been stopped so many times already by people who want to buy it. The best offer so far was twenty thousand dollars, I'm sure that number will go up over time. I still don't want to sell it.

But now that it's all done and Gene has test driven it half a dozen times, I think it's alright now. He showed me how to balance the carburetors so the engine would run like it should.

Sarah hasn't driven it yet, but she has said that she is next.

Chapter 26

Albuquerque

We had a choice between going to Grand Forks and Fargo or Albuquerque. Grand Forks is only about eighty miles south of the Canadian border. Fargo is about another eighty more. Fargo is a town of about ninety thousand, and it would be fun to talk to the people at the kit car place. But we'll wait for late spring or early summer for that visit.

By contrast, Albuquerque is about a hundred and twenty miles south of the southern Kansas line. When I vote, I always vote for the warmer areas.

Albuquerque, called the 'Queen City', has all kinds of things to do and places to go, because it is a city of more than five hundred thousand people.

It's a short flight to Denver then one to Albuquerque. We didn't have to run to get our car this time. The GSA cars were waiting when we walked into their office. Here we go, out the door and north on Wyoming Street to Central and we're there. That's the way I like it.

Kirtland Air Force Base and Sandia Labs are both housed here, but we aren't even going to look in their direction. I stamped the word 'Classified' on my brain when it comes to those places. We have no business with them and I made sure not to mention their names. You know what curiosity does.

I made reservations at the Best Western on Central. It's a good motel with a pool and near everything any of us want to see. Since the Major wants beer with every meal, I try to make sure there is some for him and that we have choices too.

I've been looking forward to our visit to the big city. I made sure our trip would coincide with the big balloon festival they have every year. It is held on the State Fairgrounds right in the middle of town on Central. The Festival is held during the Fair and there is pandemonium all around the city. There are food vendors of every kind and games for the kids as well as the grown-ups.

There is a building full of reserve units on Wyoming Street for us to inspect and harass, so we will be here for the rest of the week. I didn't want to miss any of the good stuff.

I'm always trying to slow everything down a little when it comes to the Major. The Major is like a tiger when we first arrive, then he gets settled down and becomes more normal after the first contact and opening discussions.

I have been to this city once or twice before, so I am trying to direct the guys to the best of everything I know of. The first stop for dinner tonight will be a huge Mexican restaurant called Big Jose's. They have signs plastered all over the walls about the big smothered burrito they serve. I ordered it and recommended it to the others.

It comes with beans and rice and a sopapilla and honey for dessert. Rod and Gene had the same, but the Major had a little taco plate and a big glass of beer. I don't get it. Then another big glass after that.

In the morning, we started our routine and flew through the first of the many units. I discovered later the reason the Major wanted to work so fast on it. There are balloons flying all around outside and the Major wanted to get very close to them.

There was no food on his mind when the lunch break came. We walked around the Fairgrounds for the rest of the afternoon. We stopped at a few food vendors as we walked, and of course, every beer vendor that we passed.

Rod has taken it on himself to watch the Major this trip and try to keep him out of trouble. Rod found an unused wheelchair in the back of an empty office and talked the Major into letting him push him around the park. You should see this. Too bad it doesn't have a cup holder.

The next day we found another Mexican Restaurant that advertised one of the most famous of the Mexican beers. Naturally the Major agreed with my choice. But he never orders enough food to feed a little dog. I had Huevos Rancheros. Rod and Gene had burritos and enchiladas. But the Major is still on his kick about a small taco and beer. Lots of beer.

After another long morning with one of the units and the Major has fully recovered, he is ready to attack it again.

We spent two and a half hours on this unit and only wrote up a few little things. The Major doesn't want to outbrief the unit on the same day that we do it for some reason that I haven't figured out yet. So we will start the day with that, and move on to the next one.

"Where are we going for dinner tonight, DJ?" He asked.

"I have picked out the most unusual restaurant in fifteen states for your pleasure. It is called the Louisian. I know what I'm going to have before we get there."

"It's that good?" Gene asked.

"You won't believe it."

I parked at the Louisian and we strode in like we owned the place. The waitress was there almost before we took our seats.

"What would you gents like to drink?" She said.

"Coffee. Iced tea, please. Me too. A nice cold beer for me."

"We have draught." She said.

"That's good." He said.

Once the drinks were served, she was back with her pad.

"I would like to have a big bowl of bouillabaisse."

"What did you say?" Gene said

"Give him one too, if you please."

"Well, if it's that good, I'll have on too." Rod said.

All eyes turned to the Major.

"I would like just a small sandwich and another beer please." He said. Big surprise!

I told the waitress to be sure she brought us bibs and a lot of napkins. She laughed and smiled and nodded her head.

The stew was outstanding. I like seafood any way it can be fixed. The three of us got our fill and had it all over the bibs, too.

We went for a drive around town to see the sights. The Major wanted to see something that he would remember and that he could see nowhere else. That sounds hard, but there are so many choices here, I almost couldn't boil it down. Then it came to me.

We had already been all through Old Town and I was starting the car to go back. I turned west on Central and only drove a few blocks, then turned south on Highway Forty Five.

This road isn't special in any sort of way, but I have a surprise for him. After a few blocks, I stopped at a corner.

"You know that I'm from Colorado."

"Yeah, I know." The Major said.

"And you know about that baseball field named after the beer you drink?"

He had to look at the beer can, and I couldn't help but laugh.

"Yeah, OK. So what?" He said.

"What's the name of this street?"

He craned his neck to see the street sign.

"Coors. Well I'll be." He said.

"This is Coors Boulevard. I'll bet there is not another town in this country besides the Denver area and this one with a street with that name anywhere."

That's something he won't see again.

For the rest of the week we did something different each day. And every day we had some different food each time. We drove back to the motel on Central. I wanted to go through the heart of everything again.

We passed the University of New Mexico and the State Fairgrounds and I thought, "I hope this is over soon." Driving around like a tour guide is not my favorite thing. Only two more days.

Since the Major is not from one of the western states, he doesn't understand much of the Spanish language. He has continued to ask us how to say certain things that he sees.

Being the rotten long haired hippie that I am, I told him to just put 'El' in front of the word and an 'o' on the end. All three of us have been laughing our heads off listening to him say silly things like 'el tableo'. One time when he was out of the room, I said 'el mailboxo', and all three of almost lost it. We laughed for days about that.

I was way past ready when the plane landed in Wichita. The chauffeuring and making sure that someone has fun is more than I want to do. Maybe I should get some more training and look for another job. Ya know! That sounds like a good idea.

One Saturday, soon after the car was finished, Sarah and I went for a little drive in my new old car. She has a lead foot and we were making ninety five down the freeway toward Pueblo when I noticed it and told her about it. Her foot popped off of the gas pedal and she let it coast down to the speed limit. It's a good thing there wasn't a Trooper around.

Once she got that out of her system, she drove around town like a pro. I think I made a mistake. She will want to drive it all the time now. Then it will magically become hers.

Chapter 27

Colorado Springs

It's a pretty good morning here in Wichita. Today is the first of April. Commonly known as 'April Fool's Day'. I wonder what is in store for us today.

The phone rang promptly at nine thirty, that's seven thirty Pacific Time. We all knew it was the Colonel calling with some kind of prank. He's done this before. The Major answered in his usual way.

"WRAT team, Major O'Neil speaking." He said.

He had the phone on speaker so we all could hear the conversation.

"Major, we would like your team to look at a MASH unit in Colorado Springs that is meeting in an old building previously used by the hospital there. We have been notified that the building is unsafe and would like confirmation of this. You may schedule it as soon as you can." He said.

"Colonel, you do realize what day this is and what you have suggested to us in the past?" Tim said.

"Yes. Yes. I remember. But this is on the level. I will send you special orders if you like." He said.

"Colonel, I would love that. We will get started on it today." Tim said.

"Thank you. Please send me a copy of your report when you have finished it. Good day." He said and hung up.

We worked the rest of the day on scheduling the week we would need and came up with the last week of June. There were a lot of other details to iron out but we had it all done by noon and felt pretty good about it.

"It looks like you get to visit home on this trip, DJ." Gene said.

"Yes and I can show you guys some really fine food and all the tourist attractions. But be careful of my mother, she will want to adopt all of you and mother you. That's just the way she is."

Later in the day I called Dad and told him what was in the plan. Mom, of course, was on the other phone. "You picked a perfect time. The Academy graduation is in that week. And the Gazette had an article about a big fly-over that they will have. Lots of planes in an air parade. Then later there will be the big air show at Pete Field where the public will be allowed to go into some special planes parked on the runway." She said. "I'm excited about the air show and you coming!"

She didn't need to say that. I know how she is about planes. She should have been in the Air Force. But, if she had been, she'd still be in now if it was up to her.

It was a short flight from Wichita to the Springs and there were GSA cars waiting for us.

"I know of a fantastic place to stay, the Apollo Park Suites. I've stayed there before and it is great!"

The Major wanted to do an initial look at this place that the MASH was in since it was early in the day. I drove to Fort Carson and the gate guard gave us directions to the right building.

"It certainly is an old building." Tim said. "We need to find someone and have them let us inside."

Once inside, it didn't look any better.

"Your unit meets here every week?" Tim asked. "It looks like it could fall down any minute."

"It's not that bad, but it would be nice if we could get into the new hospital. It's just not ready for us yet, they said." The AST said.

"We will be back tomorrow and we'll write our report before we leave." The Major said.

We spent most of the day with the preliminaries and now it was time for a good home-cooked meal. Dad was sitting in a chair in the living room reading the paper, but Mom was waiting for us. I don't know how she does it.

"DJ, I'm so glad to see you." She hugged me and began again with the guys. "Hello boys, you're just in time for dinner. Are you hungry? It's all ready now." She said and ushered each one of them to a chair where the table had been set and ready.

It was a long day and we gorged ourselves on Mom's dinner.

Mom told them all about the Academy graduation and what the Gazette article said about the planes at Pete field and the flyover and she insisted that we be there to see it all. She wants us to get a place to park on the Academy so she can be close to the flyover and get a good look at the planes. I know her better than she thinks I do.

Tim and the guys looked at me and I shrugged my shoulders at them. Tim finally said. "Mrs. McAllister, why don't you ride with us to the Academy and we can all get a good close look at the flyover. It should be something to see."

Boy was he right there. We finished the report on Tuesday and mailed a copy to the Colonel.

We all laid around the house Wednesday till she said it was time to go. I drove very fast up I-25 to the Academy and onto the base. Mom has a lot of redeeming qualities, but one of them is not punctuality.

I found a spot on Stadium Boulevard so we could be out of the van and see everything. It wasn't long before we saw the first planes in the parade. A couple of F-16's were leading the parade, followed by an F-111 Fighter Bomber, a B-52 the biggest bomber. There was a B-1 painted in Army green. You should have heard what they had to say about that. At the end there were a couple of others that I didn't recognize. I wasn't in the Air Force.

Just as the B-1 got close to some of the buildings, it dipped down to a very low level and buzzed the whole area. I'll bet the windows shook in those buildings.

At the very end were two black helicopters running nearly together. Of course Mom has been jumping up and down the whole time and waving to the planes. Suddenly she stopped and began waving at the helos.

"He waved at me!" She screamed. "He waved at me!"

"Who waved at you?"

"The guy in the helicopter waved at me!" She yelled.

"Oh Mom, come on! How could he have seen you?"

To this day she has maintained that whoever was in the helo waved at her. Later she read in the paper that the President gave the address at the graduation, and she was positive that it was him that waved at her.

I took a short run around the Academy so that they all could see the static planes that were placed around the grounds. One of them is painted all up in Thunderbird colors. We had to stop and get out there so they could touch it. The big black B-52 was a favorite of all of them, so we stopped there too.

We spent the rest of the day going through small, large and gi-huge-ic planes at Peterson field and again she was out of her mind with joy.

On the way back to their house, I drove to my house and picked up Doreen. The guys absolutely had to go inside and look it all over.

"This is your house, DJ?" Tim asked.

"Yes, but Doreen lives here and takes care of it."

"How do you pay for it?" He asked.

"It's only eighty three dollars a month. Surely I can set that much aside for my sister."

Chapter 28

Bowling With Sarah

Between building my new car and going out of town with three other guys, I have tried to meet and become friendly with everyone I can locally. One day, a few months ago, a Sergeant at the Arcom asked me to do a favor for him.

He wanted me to fill-in for him on a bowling team. I haven't been bowling in a league since I was sixteen. I told him that I wasn't sure that I could do it anymore. He, of course, poo-pooed that and said that he was sure I could. So I went a little early that first night to find where I was going. I was twenty-four years old and didn't have sense enough to come in out of the rain, but I did learn something valuable there.

If I want information, I would rather ask a woman than a man for several reasons. I would rather listen to a girl's voice than a man's anytime. I can follow what she's saying a lot better and there's no ego to deal with. Also, while she is talking to me, I can enjoy looking at her beautiful form as well. Oh, look. Here comes a looker now.

"Excuse me, I'm DJ McAllister and I'm the new substitute on the 'Pin Slingers' team, can you tell me where I can find the team?" I asked her.

"Sure, I'm Linda Williams. See there." she said pointing across the room, "That guy with the glasses, talking to the blonde girl, that's them." She said.

Linda is a beautiful statuesque thin woman about five foot nine and one or two years older than I am, with blonde over-the-shoulder length hair. I would have asked Linda for a date until I saw the rings on her finger. Out of the corner of my eye I could see another girl walking toward us.

"Oh, here comes Sarah, my best friend, she and a couple of guys are on our team." She said with a big smile building on her face.

Linda introduced her friend. As Sarah extended her hand in my direction for me to shake hands, I took her hand and was going to say something, but I realized my whole body has quit, frozen in time, seized up, nothing worked. Now the smile on Linda's face is ear to ear.

Her hand was so soft and she was so beautiful that my heart stopped, my lungs quit working, and my mouth went dry. It was like something flowed out of her hand into mine and I stopped when I looked at her. I couldn't talk. I tried, but just some weird sounds came out. I have known a lot of beautiful girls, but Sarah was head and shoulders above all of them. And I was overwhelmed by her beauty. Now Linda is actually laughing.

Finally I croaked out something and Linda and Sarah both laughed and pushed me toward the guy she pointed out earlier. She was saying something about getting started. I could hear them giggling behind me and I felt a little humiliated as I stumbled toward the alley where my new team was standing.

It took me a couple of months during that bowling season for me to learn how to talk again when I approached Sarah to try to say something. I made it my goal that when our team finally played Sarah's team, I would find some reason, any reason, to talk to her between frames. I don't understand what is happening. I have never had these kinds of problems when I talked with girls before.

Eventually, after several months, she gave me her phone number just before the bowling league year was over. That was the beginning of a lot of wonderful times for us.

Over the years I have had several girlfriends, but none like Sarah. My first real love is Sarah. She is the best thing that ever happened to me. She is everything that I am not. She is polished, I'm rough. She could cook and take care of the house, I'd be starving and living in a pig sty. She is a beautiful caring woman.

This job of mine is pretty good and so is the pay. We pretty much get to set our own hours as long as the inspections get done. We work a lot of overtime when we're out of town on a trip, which means we get a lot of time off when we're home. That part's good, but the traveling gets under your skin after a while. Especially when you have a sweet woman in your life and you wish to be in her presence.

It is like that with Sarah. She and I spend many long hours discussing our goals in life, wants, needs, and children. I just always want to be near her, and finally the day came when I proposed marriage. Even then, I didn't know if she would accept. She would be the gift that would complete me. It was a day of celebration and two happy people would become one on that day.

Sarah and I had decided before we were married to have two children and then we would see if we wanted more when the youngest was three years old. We had talked about having another baby when Harry was three, but decided to wait one more year.

Before I had met Sarah, I had already bought a small bungalow style home with a basement on Pattie Street in Wichita. It had one medium and two small bedrooms. Once we were married, I tore out some walls and made one large bedroom with a private bath and one medium bedroom out of it. I added a fireplace in the living room and built a two car garage back by the alley. We keep her car and my Woodie in it. I did a few other additions to the house and grounds that I could actually do.

We used to make love in front of a roaring fire in the living room pretty often during the winter months. She thought the house was a castle. There are pictures of us are all over the walls in every room. There is a big one of her in the bedroom where I can see it every day and every night.

As soon as you walk in, you could tell a woman lives there because of the woman's touches all through the house in the decorating. My clothes and junk are piled all around when I get home and the house looks cluttered. She fusses at me about that when she cleans it up. But I'm learning and it will get better eventually.

A lot of my stuff is on the shelves around the house. I have always enjoyed designing buildings. I wanted to go to college to be an architect, but the Service thought I was an Electronics Technician, so it never happened. I started building little model buildings a long time ago and now there are a lot of shelves displaying my models all around the house.

We had the best little baby, Harry. Sarah did all the work and I only sat in the waiting room wringing my hands. I didn't realize how fast little babies became little people.

Sarah does everything for Harry and I, cooking, cleaning, taking care of the house, paying the bills. She does it all smiling, singing and dancing around the house like she was in a movie or something. And all this packaged in a five foot six inch, freckle-faced redhead with a terrific figure.

Sarah and I got real lucky when her mother told her to go see Mrs. Johnson. Mrs. Johnson has known Sarah since she was born. She has a warm smile and reminds me of everyone's grandmother. She lives just down our street three blocks. She has been a friend of Sarah's mother for many years.

Sometimes Sarah would take our son, Harry, and go shopping, but if she was in a hurry, she would leave him with Mrs. Johnson for a couple of hours. Harry loved it and loved Mrs. Johnson.

I keep my special little new old car in the garage at the rear of the lot with my pickup. Every time Sarah comes over to my house she wants to go for a "little" ride in it. Now she drives her car to the driveway at the rear, parks it out of the way, and always finds a reason for her to drive the Woodie.

I had to make her a key of her own so she could drive it when the team is out of town on a trip.

Any little trip to see Linda or shopping or visiting friends or relatives requires the car's help. She even drives it and me to church on Sunday. She has fallen hard for that car.

I don't get much of a chance to drive my little Woody. I don't think I want to build another one. It took months of time and a ton of money to finish it. But if that's what it takes to make her happy, I'll do it.

Not The End